PSIONIC

YOUR THOUGHTS ARE NOT YOUR OWN.

PSIONIC

YOUR THOUGHTS ARE NOT YOUR OWN.

MICHAEL DAVID

SOLASTA
PRESS

an imprint of
THE OGHMA PRESS

OGHMA

CREATIVE MEDIA

Bentonville, Arkansas • Los Angeles, California
www.oghmacreative.com

Library of Congress Cataloging-in-Publication Data

Names: David, Michael, author.
Title: Dimensions/Michael David. | Dimensions #1
Description: First Edition. | Bentonville: Solasta, 2022.
Identifiers: LCCN: | ISBN: 978-1-63373-635-1 (trade paperback) | ISBN: 978-1-63373-636-8 (eBook)
Subjects: | BISAC: FICTION/Thrillers/Supernatural | FICTION/Thrillers/Psychological | FICTION/Thrillers/Suspense
LC record available at: https://lccn.loc.gov/

Solasta Press trade paperback edition May, 2021

Cover & Interior Design by Casey W. Cowan
Editing by George "Clay" Mitchell

Published by Solasta Press, an imprint of The Oghma Press, a subsidiary of The Oghma Book Group.

This book is dedicated to Janet, my wife and best friend.
I couldn't have done this without you!

THIS COULDN'T HAVE HAPPENED WITHOUT the help of my critique group buddies. Sincere thanks to Jodi, Linda, and Taylor. You're the best!

HERE, PIGGY, PIGGY

ALLEN COSTAS, THE DIRECTOR OF PSYCHIC Espionage, hands me a check for five million dollars, and my life hits bottom. As in, totally, rock bottom.

Happy friggin' birthday, Archer Wilson. This bitchin' day can't get any worse.

The scorching Texas sun slices through Dad's study window and glints off the glass of bourbon I'd poured for Costas. He slurps his drink, looking like Charlie Sheen after a weekend frat party. The director's wig, with a snarky comb over, is complemented by his pink, turned up nose and two obvious nostrils.

Uh-huh. A pig with a wig.

He jerks his necktie and waddles around a pile of packing boxes.

"Archer, it's your twenty-first birthday today, and I know what you're thinking. It's a bitch right now. But your parents often said, God won't give you more than you can handle."

The bastard's in my mind. Heat blasts across my face and I step in close. "Costas, whoever wrote that piece of crap was smoking crack." I stab my finger into his chest and look down at him. "I'm not in your psychic incision class anymore, so stay the hell out of my mind!"

I squash the check into a tight ball. Shove it in his drink. Stir it with my finger. "Your death money won't bring my parents back. So, screw yourself."

His lips snap shut and his double chin quivers.

This little piggy is too gutless to speak his mind, but the rage in his eye's squeals *fuckyoufuckyoufuckyou!* All the way home.

I reach over and grab the two crematory urns on Dad's desk. Adrenaline mainlines my system and my heart bucks to one-hundred miles-per-hour. Both hands shake as I clutch my parents' cremains.

"Do me a favor and man up. Grow something in that baby boy underwear that'd make your Momma proud."

I'm so close to him, I smell his Dollar Store cologne. "My parents were involved in psychic espionage. In a secure government facility. So, how the hell did they die?"

He uncoils to his full height, but still has to look up at me.

"You blame me for your parent's deaths, Archer. I understand that. But Mike and Janet were my friends, too." A nervous tic lifts the corner of his mouth.

"I've reviewed the closed-circuit footage of their deaths a hundred times. Security measures were being followed. To the letter. As much as I'd like to tell you the details, I'm sworn to secrecy."

"You've got to be kidding." My voice invokes all the charm of fingernails on a chalk board.

Costas refuses to look at the two urns in my hands. Instead, he glares at me.

"Shit-can the thousand-yard-stare. Both my parents are gone. Dying at the same freakin' place. At a job they couldn't talk about. In your facility."

The pig with a wig moves closer, reaches out to touch my shoulder. A calculated effort to comfort me. It's too late for that. I jerk away.

He shrugs. "For a young woman, Archer, you've got balls, and you're damned strong. In my business, power and psychic ability are what separates the one percent from the masses. You've got both. That's why you were at the top of my psychic training classes. That's why you and your five classmates have been groomed for our program. And that's why I want you to replace your parents."

I psychically tune-in to the emotions within his mind—a toxic sludge of guilt, grief, and a gallon of gall. He's hiding something. I know it. But I just can't focus.

Something dark and sharp hitches up my throat. "Get out of our house. Leave. Before I do something stupid."

His shoulders slump and he jiggles away. All three hundred pounds of him.

Just as he grips the doorknob, I spin around. "I will never work for you. *Ever.*"

His eyes darken, obscuring a private agenda. "Never say never, Archer. Things are in motion. Motion that can't be stopped."

He opens the front door and a wave of Texas heat rolls in as he leaves.

The clock on the marble mantle goes snick, snick, snick, snipping the time away. I hear a car door slam. Children's voices drift upon the wind.

Why do I feel like I'm drowning, and don't know it?

FIFTEEN MINUTES LATER, I STILL HAVEN'T deciphered Costas' message. Things are in motion might mean the project Mom and Dad worked on. But what is it that can't be stopped? Where do I fit in this puzzle?

Critical pieces of information are missing. I take a

deep breath and engage the psychic mechanism I've used since childhood.

Give me guidance.

The words drop into my subconscious and I close my eyes, preparing a receptive mental state.

An image forms in my mind's eye. Explodes into something I never expected. My vision shows an old rotary dial phone.

Black, like Mother's. An antiquated technology from another era.

Cherished by Mother. The phone she'd refused to replace.

Used by Mother. The same one I'd disconnected an hour ago.

I open my eyes and look to the left. Mom's old rotary dial phone sits on a stack of boxes, waiting to be packed.

The first ring is sharp and unmistakable. Each successive ring grows in volume and shrillness. I stare dumbly at the phone. This can't be happening.

It's still disconnected!

I pick up the plastic hand piece. Unnatural coolness against my palm. My hand shakes. I sit down at the desk. Put the receiver to my ear. I don't have a clue what to say. Finally, "Archer here."

A series of clicks and faint whistling travels down the line. Followed by what sounds like insects scuttling across glass. Then, a silence bursts open, so deep it hurts my ear.

I hear a woman's faint sigh. My knuckles ache from gripping the receiver. "Anybody there?"

Happy Birthday, Archer.

It feels like Dwayne Johnson body slams my chest. I can't catch my breath.

This is some kinda sick joke. "Who the hell are you?"

Your mother, Archer.

The Rock just rolled over my chest.

Again.

I'm talking to a dead person on a dead line.

Confusion and disbelief ravage my psyche. But a glimmer of hope breaks through my turmoil.

"M-Mom?"

Archer, listen to me. Leave now. Go to our cabin. Do not trust anyone.

"But Mom, how can you…? We had your funeral last week. You and Dad. The ashes are right here, in front of me."

They want you, Archer. They will take you. They will torture you. Just to make us cooperate.

"Mom, who are they? What's going on?"

I can't explain. Not now. Please, honey. Just go.

My mind switches gears. How long will I be gone? How much money to take? How much to pack?

Focus, Archer! You don't have time to pack. Grab the Beemer keys and go. Now!

I gnaw my bottom lip. Because I'm talking to my Mother, trusting this voice on the phone that sounds just like hers. Plus, she knows what I'm thinking.

"All right, but what's going on?"

I'll tell you when you get there. But hurry. They'll be sending someone you don't want to meet. Le Cadavre. He's ruthless.

There is a long pause.

Call 273-7123 before you leave town. A sleep specialist, Dr. Navarro, has a package for you—something to help in the next few days. I love you Archer. Remember your training.

I bolt upright.

The line is silent now, and I tuck the phone under my arm. Grab the Beemer keys and run for the door.

Happy friggin' birthday to me.

I'M INHALING YOUR SCENT

LE CADAVRE STOOD IN THE GUTTED country church, a church that he'd delivered unto darkness so thick, so total, Satan would have wept for joy.

It was a place where he'd ignored the stench of spilled blood. Ignored desperate pleas. Ignored his victim's screams.

It was a place of cruelty and darkness.

A place the devil called home.

He took a deep breath and moved through the fabric of unholiness. Far from his presence, unseen hands tripped a switch and birthed a shaft of brilliance. Brilliance that shone from the church rafters above, bathing a small area where the pulpit had once stood. But he knew that no amount of light could dispel the blackness within his soul.

Stepping bare-footed into the sterile circle of light, he touched his choppy, silver hair—hair that was stylishly severe and swept back from his broad forehead. Bare from the waist up, he wore baggy work pants, and the large, black-rimmed glasses on his nose only enhanced the coldness in his eyes. He had studied his image and crafted a persona meant to intimidate.

Le Cadavre shifted, and cool leather straps bit into the puffy, white flesh of his shoulders. Extending halfway down his torso, they were secured by a circular band that completed an abbreviated harness. An AM transistor radio rested in the middle of his chest, held by the parallel straps.

His breathing was slow and relaxed, causing a faint ripple upon the living darkness. He calmly inserted a nipple ring and clipped a bare, seven-inch wire to the metallic band, forming a crude, nine-inch antenna with an adapter on the end that brushed against his skin.

Connecting it to the radio, Le Cadavre thought about the past two years. The secluded country church that had offered the privacy he demanded. The discreet negotiations. The final confirmation that it was his.

He then brutally smothered the spirit of this church, a beacon of hope that no longer shone within this house of darkness. The pews and Bibles were removed as well as all that was sacred or symbolic, until only a shell remained.

To ensure total privacy, he nailed heavy, black drapes over the stained-glass windows. Even though the sanctuary was five miles from the nearest habitant, his cautious nature was fueled by paranoia. A trickle of sweat ran down his upper lip as he looked straight ahead. Costas's instructions had been unusual. Le Cadavre was told to wait for a call. A call from Archer's dead mother, Janet Wilson. A call on an unplugged rotary dial phone.

Interesting.

A minute later, the unconnected phone rang.

He picked up the receiver. "Missus Wilson, I've been expecting your call. May I address you as Janet?" Le Cadavre cleared his throat. "You know I've been retained by the facility to ensure the safety of your daughter."

In other words, make sure Mike and I cooperate.

Le Cadavre smiled slightly, even though Janet couldn't see him. "Costas told me that you and your husband have been misbehaving. Obviously, neither of you have his interests in mind." He chuckled. "Just think how useful your new abilities would be in the right hands."

The psychic espionage program has rectal cancer, and Costas is the asshole.

"Janet, it's not too late to correct your indiscretion. You know, start fresh. Clean slate, if you will."

Don't patronize me. There's too much at stake to turn back. Costas must be stopped.

Le Cadavre toyed with the phone cord, wrapping it around his finger, tugging it lightly. "I don't care what Costas has in mind. But I do have a delightful surprise for you."

He slowly reached into his pants pocket and removed a turquoise scarf. "Janet, I know you can't see me, but I'm holding your scarf. The same one you wore on the day of your presumptive death. So, listen closely, I'm about to share something special with you."

He tilted his head and moved the fabric under his nose like a wine connoisseur assessing a fine wine. "I'm inhaling your scent."

Total bliss.

"I know things about you, Janet."

You. Don't. Know. Me.

"Oh, but I do," he whispered, "I know what happened in that vacant house so many years ago."

A nervous silence ensued.

"The two-story vacant house, Janet. Summer of 1994?" Le Cadavre listened closely. He could almost hear the harsh scrape and scrabble of her hidden fear.

Burn in Hell, you freak!

"Good. Janet. Now you remember. Pity you never told the police. Never told your husband, Mike. Never told Archer. Now, did you? After that horrific night, you conceived. Prayed that Archer was Mike's child. But in the darkest corner of your mind, you knew the truth."

Janet stifled a cry.

"You. Don't. Know. Me." He mimicked her words without warmth. "But I really do."

I never told anyone about the rape. Janet cried into the telephone.

He lowered the scarf, dropped it on the floor. "You see, I have a special gift. Unique, even among psychometrists. In the paranormal world, psychometry is the ability to hold personal objects, and gain knowledge about their history."

Le Cadavre thought he heard Janet's fear, ripping and tearing and screaming to get out of its box. He held his breath for a moment and exhaled. "My gift separates me from the norm, because I can discern the intimate, tragic events my prey holds by smelling their scent on personal clothing. I can even connect when I detect perspiration in the air. I'm a psychic bloodhound, Janet. I uncover the history of personal trauma and dark secrets we all possess. No one is safe from me. Not even you."

You sorry bastard.

"All Costas wants, my dear, is for you and Mike to come back into the fold. You can make it easy, or you can make it hard. Only you can decide. But when I have your precious daughter, your bargaining power is gone. You will do what Costas says, or Archer will pay the price."

He sensed Janet reaching inside to summon all that was strong and true.

It will be a fine day in hell before Mike and I come back. And don't discount Archer. I've trained her in things you never imagined.

"If that's true, so be it."

Your pathetic threats can't change my mind. You have no idea how much power Mike and I have, and it's growing stronger. So, tell Costas to go fuck himself. And fuck you, too.

"Indulge me for a moment." Le Cadavre thumbed his

transistor radio dial on his chest. The stations blared and receded until he settled on one, then turned the volume up so Janet could hear. "I want to introduce you to some old-time-gospel, Brother Hell style."

The radio blasted out its tinny sound, *The time of the Lord is near, and I ask you, are you ready! Ready to account for your sins?*

Le Cadavre moved the dial slightly, connected to an adjacent station. "Now, listen to the Rush Limbaugh wannabe."

In these times of liberal spending, be prepared for more chaos. Between the President and his henchmen, can you survive the coming economic crisis?

"I trust you listened, Janet. And like the infomercials say, 'But wait, there's more.'"

He moved the dial until it was between the two stations. "In the old days, it wasn't uncommon for two close AM stations to bleed over, fading from one broadcast to the other."

The tiny radio delivered its message, *And we will take an eye for an eye, and a tooth for a tooth.* The minister's voice rose in fervor, then faded out.

The financial guru cut back in. *In this current financial situation, take as much as you can.*

"I'm called Le Cadavre for a reason, Janet, and precious Archer will pay for your rebellion. When I have her under my control, the fun will begin. You see, the words of the two broadcasts will offer direction to our encounter. When the voices fade in and out from the two programs, they're telling me what to do. If Archer were here, I might take an eye or a tooth. Or I might take all that I can. Regardless, I will be guided by the voices to perform what I do best."

He waited for a response. Was greeted by silence. He gently put the receiver down. The next few days would surely test his abilities.

But Le Cadavre lived for a challenge.

3

MY POOR HEART

I END MY CELL PHONE CALL as I blast down the desolate, Texas highway at one-hundred miles-per-hour. Sammy Hagar's "I Can't Drive Fifty-Five" pounds through the car's speakers. The poetic justice isn't lost on me as I rip up the asphalt on the way to our ranch cabin.

The wooden fence posts zip by, and I can't help but think of the bizarre contact from Mother. Being psychic, I constantly stretch my definition of reality. Things that I can't logically explain occur frequently. When the result of a psychic hit resonates in a deeper realm, it lives outside of the thinking mind. If you trust that inner sense of knowing, then acceptance grows from your intuitive perceptions. Faith in my psychic impressions ultimately wins over my logical mind.

In the case of receiving calls on a disconnected phone and speaking to my dead mother, well this requires a greater leap on my part. Not impossible, but definitely a stretch.

Then, there is the package I just picked up from Dr. Navarro—a special brain-wave induction device specially designed by my dead mother. It rests on my passenger seat and is composed of a battery-powered control box, black sunglasses with one red, LED light on the inside of each lens, and headphones.

When I met Navarro twenty minutes ago, he was quick to tell me that he had been shut out of dream research, due to his theory that dreams are entry points into the multiverse. He currently worked as a technician for a sleep clinic and pursued his unorthodox belief in a cluttered workshop at home.

The device he had designed for mother would stimulate the brain through a special pattern of light and sound, designed to help the user find the right frequency to enter another dimension.

All this is fine and dandy, but I don't have a clue what Mom wants me to do with it.

I adjust the AC vent and glance at her phone on the passenger floorboard. The dash clock shows a bit after six p.m., and when I look up, the evening light glares in my eyes. I flip the sun visor down, and a picture flutters into my lap face up.

A one second glance is all it takes for my heart to go squishy. It's the last picture of Mom and Dad and me, together. Alive.

I look up from the picture because the images are too raw and painful. Dad, with his black hair beginning to gray at the temples. Mom, with her thick, brown ponytail. Dad, with his chiseled jaw line. Mom, in her pressed linen blouse.

Mom's leaning against Dad's shoulder, looking young and vibrant. Her face radiant with the crazy love she had for him.

I'm standing in front of my parents in this picture and the top of my head nearly reaches theirs. It looks like they're about to choke me, they're hugging so tight.

My long brown hair is swept back from my forehead, and I'm wearing my favorite classic-rock tee shirt. It's easy to see that I got Mom's sky-blue eyes and Dad's fair skin. It's all too easy to see that I'm grinning like a fool. I got that from their total, unconditional love.

Without warning, the combined brute force of The Rock and Vin Diesel, collides against my heart. It's a nightmare, tag team sensation that pummels and smashes and slams and stomps the life from my chest. It's the kickass, leading men of Hollywood, versus moi.

I'm losing this battle on so many levels.

Are Mom and Dad really alive?

4

TEN MILLIGRAMS ONCE DAILY

COSTAS LISTENED TO LE CADAVRE ON a secure line and took a gut shot from the panic in his subordinate's voice.

"I'm inside the house, now, and Archer is gone. Nothing was taken. No clothes, no food, no credit cards. The bitch left in a hurry. And the front door was open when I got here."

Costas took a deep breath. "Focus for me. How long has she been gone?"

"Judging by her scent, thirty minutes, tops."

The facility director was exquisitely aware of Le Cadavre's psychic gifts and would use any opportunity to squeeze intel from that ability. "Were you able to pick up any psychic information on her? Any weakness or emotional trauma?"

There was a long beat. *"No. I mean—damn it. This has never happened before. There's nothing. Absolutely nothing! That's what has me rattled."*

The director groaned. "Seems Miss Archer is as resourceful as her mother. But she made a mistake. Thirty minutes ago, she called Dr. Manuel Navarro, a disgraced dream researcher, to ask a question about a device she picked up from him."

"And?"

"Find out what it was."

"The cell tap paid off."

Costas ignored the compliment. "The good Doctor will be there for the evening. I suggest you pay him a visit. Then figure out where Archer is going."

Le Cadavre took a deep breath.

"I'll deliver her, and your worries will be over." Costas' enforcer paused for a moment. *"There is one thing I found, something odd."*

"What's that?"

"A recent prescription in Archer's bathroom—an empty bottle of Zyprexa. I did a Google search on my cell, and get this, it's an antipsychotic used to treat heavy-duty mental disorders."

"You've done well."

"There's more. I found Archer's personal diary, pinpointing her first psychotic break. Happened a bit over three years ago. And you're gonna love this, she's schizophrenic."

"Give me a second." Costas went silent, did the calculation, "Today's her twenty-first birthday, so the hospitalization occurred when she was eighteen. Was there a date on her diary entry?"

"June third, three years ago."

"Archer's been in my psychic training program for a year. She apparently lied on the initial application, and the subsequent background check missed it."

"That's possible. With the training program's low security clearance, it wouldn't have merited a deeper investigation."

"Bring her prescription bottle and diary."

"I have them already."

"Good. Find the Doctor. Find out where Archer went. Then, we'll find a skillet and fry her frickin' ass."

5

THE MAGIC 8 BALL

PERSPIRATION BROKE OUT ON DR. MANUEL Navarro's brow as his visitor, John Ford, sat in a hard, plastic chair positioned in front of Navarro's walnut desk.

Comfort would have dictated that he should have upholstered, plush seating, but he had purposefully chosen the bare-bones furniture. Because of that action, and several others, he prayed that none of his visitors suspected his ulterior motive. If discovered, it would expose his greatest weakness and damage his credibility.

Quite simply, he couldn't deal with human beings. Didn't like being around them. Didn't like to talk with them. Simply put, he didn't like people.

His first defense mechanism to speed their exit was to seat his audience in uncomfortable chairs. Because, once they started squirming, it wasn't long before they left. He reached into his lower desk drawer and removed his second line of defense, a Magic 8 Ball. The original Magic 8 Ball was used as a fortune telling device. It was up to the user to turn the clear, plastic window down—then ask a yes or no question.

When the 8 Ball was turned up, the twenty-sided die inside would float to the top and display an answer. He would repeat the generic phrase and minimize his social interaction.

As he sat behind his desk, he engaged his final defense mechanism—he turned the room heat up to a sweltering, eighty-five degrees with his iPhone.

His visitor, a stocky, white-haired man, leaned forward. "I have some questions for you, Doctor."

Navarro held the 8 Ball low in his lap, out of sight, and turned it up. The die floated to the top and he read the words slowly, "Yes, definitely."

"A friend of mine was just here. Archer Wilson."

Navarro tipped the device once more. "Concentrate and ask again."

The visitor's face went blank and the room was suddenly quiet. Navarro was in deep, now. The blood rushed from his face as he frantically searched for something to say. Seconds ticked by. Sweat trickled down his neck and back. Fear crippled him.

His palms were slick with perspiration and his heart *tump, tump,* tumbled in his chest. The room smelled like nervous sweat, and he wondered for the thousandth time, why he was so terrified of human interaction? He'd read every self-help book in print and was still at a loss to explain his affliction. He couldn't understand his fear.

JOHN FORD, AKA LE CADAVRE, SAT in the hard-plastic chair and let Navarro's stress build as he observed him. The Doctor, he noted, was brutally handsome in a way most women dreamed about. Dark eyes reflected an innate intelligence and suggested a sharp intellect. Even his grooming and presence inspired confidence.

Le Cadavre sniffed the air again and knew that appearances could also be deceiving. He flashed a cagey smile.

Navarro forced his hands behind his head and stiffened in his chair.

Le Cadavre spoke softly, "The young lady who was just here, Archer Wilson, well, both her parents recently died at a government facility. So sad, losing a mother and father like that. I work at a different department there and was acquainted with Mike and Janet. I tried to contact Archer at home, but she wasn't in. I know it might sound trite, but I'm worried about her."

Navarro arched an eyebrow. "She was here about thirty minutes ago, then phoned in a question about a product I sold her. Archer told me that she was on the way to their family's vacation home outside of Amarillo. A small ranch house. Said she needed to sort through her feelings."

"That's understandable." Le Cadavre leaned forward. "Would you have her phone number at the ranch house?

Navarro hesitated a moment. "The only number I have on my caller ID is from her cell. However, I'm not comfortable giving it out to anyone, without her permission. Nor, am I comfortable discussing my business with her. How did you know she came here?"

"She mentioned your name to a friend, who knew I was concerned about Archer's state of mind."

While talking with Navarro, he had thumbed in Archer's family name in directory assistance and gotten an address for their country home.

Now, it was time to unleash the Doctor's inner demons.

Le Cadavre steepled his fingers. "I appreciate your ethics, and I would like to reciprocate with a few personal observations. 'First, your choice of furniture is interesting. As well as the stifling temperature in this room. I believe both have an ulterior motive behind them."

Dr. Navarro's eyes opened wide.

"It appears to me that you have a painful flaw, one that you don't understand. And you have done your best to camouflage it with some ingenious tools." Navarro glanced at the black plastic sphere in his lap. "I must say, the Magic 8 Ball is pure genius. Quite effective and comforting for you."

Anger twisted Navarro's face. "Who are you? How the hell do you know these things?"

"I am just an individual. One who has a unique gift. However, I'm here to state the reasons behind your behavior. As an educated man, you've studied psychology and are aware of certain paranormal abilities, specifically psychometry?"

Dr. Navarro nodded, not certain where this was going.

"I'm a psychometrist on steroids—because I can discern buried emotional trauma from a personal scent."

The Doctor's eyes reflected skepticism, which was not lost on Le Cadavre.

"How else would I know what you've hidden from your friends and customers for years?" He cocked his head. "Do you know why you developed these defense mechanisms?"

Navarro broke eye contact. "No! Damn it. I don't."

"I do, and I'm going to provide you a rare insight." The corners of his lips lifted in anticipation. "What do you remember about your mother?"

Navarro jerked. "She left right after I was born."

"Is that what you were told? Or do you remember recurring fragments of her in your dreams? Dreams that feel too real. Perhaps, buried memories of when you were two?"

"Get out!" Navarro slammed the desk with his fist. "Or I'll throw you out."

"Bear with me for a moment." Le Cadavre smiled indulgently. "Because I know how to unlock your fear of human contact and give you the understanding you crave."

Navarro glared at him.

"Your mother did not leave you after birth. No, my friend, she was alive and present for almost two years after that. At that tender age, you experienced a profound trauma that blocked the memory of her as effectively as if she had really left." He leaned forward in the plastic chair. "You still relive in your dream fragments the caustic interaction between your parents. The horrible fights between two immature teenagers not prepared to raise a young child." He spread his hands. "Here is the key to your dilemma, Doctor. At the tender age of two, you witnessed the final confrontation. Your parents' emotions were out of control that night, the fighting and screaming so overpowering that your father strangled your mother while you looked on. I would even say you have a dark, violent side you've tried hard to suppress."

Defiance travelled across Navarro's face. Twisted to confusion. Turned into total terror.

"Your young mind was not prepared for what you witnessed. However, you formed a connection then that is still in place today. The child in you knew human contact could get you killed. And in that childlike reasoning, person-to-person interaction has always been the enemy. It was to be avoided at all costs. Wouldn't you agree?"

Navarro leaned back in his chair and put his hands over his eyes. His shoulders shook, and Le Cadavre knew that the Doctor cried for the little boy who'd lost his mother, as well as for the shell of a man that he'd become.

Minutes passed in silence until Navarro finally composed himself. He took a tissue from the box on his desk and dried his face.

"I have delivered you to a much kinder place, Doctor, one that you never knew existed."

Yet, it would have been equally rewarding to destroy

the Doctor, just by exposing his defense mechanisms and repressed anger. But Le Cadavre lived in an internal balancing act with his psychic ability. For each evil action he committed, he was compelled to use his psychic ability for good. These opposing forces were internally tallied, and the sum of each part would evolve into a greater whole. Very soon, the total from each part would reach a critical mass. When that moment came, he would become like his former victims, totally powerless, with a look on his face that begged for deliverance. Not knowing why, he longed for that which would destroy him.

Le Cadavre stood to leave. "I trust that our chat has been helpful?

Navarro looked him straight in the eyes and appeared as if he'd gone nine rounds with his greatest fear. His face twisted from raw emotion, yet a terrible weight had been lifted from his shoulders. He nodded slightly.

"You wouldn't mind if I keep your 8 Ball, Doctor? As a... memento of our time together?"

Navarro laid it on the desk. "Be my guest. I have a feeling I won't be needing it anymore."

For a moment, Le Cadavre basked in the innocent glow of the Doctor's new understanding. Even though the internal balance between good and evil was now even, he knew the dark force would build once again and be unleashed against the unsuspecting Archer Wilson.

That thought turned him on more than he could explain.

6

HE LIVES ONE BLOCK FROM THE TWILIGHT ZONE

IT IS PITCH BLACK AS I wind my way over the dirt road, leading to my parents' prairie cabin. A fresh grassland scent filters through my cracked window, allowing the cool night breeze to mix with the warmer air inside. Overhead, I glimpse the diamond-like glitter of sparkling stars.

My car thermometer registers a comfortable sixty-five degrees outside as I turn onto the cabin's driveway. When I stop, the motion detector light flashes on, and continues to shine while I unlock the front door. As I open the creaking door, I have no luggage, thanks to Mom's instructions, and only carry her black rotary phone and Dr. Navarro's device. I flip the overhead light on and walk down the short entry-way, then make a left into the living room, where I adjust the thermostat and turn on a few table lamps.

A cheery glow lights the room where Mom and Dad recently installed new furniture. I drop onto an overstuffed couch in front of the stone fireplace. A handcrafted aspen coffee table sits in front of my knees and holds something distinctly odd. A small plastic box, roughly the size of a brick, with a small indentation on the top at each end.

It takes me a moment, as I look at the mechanism, to realize what it's for. I pick up Mom's rotary handset and place the earpiece and mouthpiece snugly in both hollows. Looking at this weird setup, I don't have a clue what it does, though, the coincidence of this device being in place brings a stab of recognition in my gut. Mom, Dad, and I were here four weeks ago, and by leaving this device, Mom must have had some idea of the events that would lead me back.

A small, green light flickers on at the box's base, and the unplugged, rotary phone rings once. Then, a pinging sound, like a computer connection being forged, blasts from our home theatre surround sound. The seventy-inch flat screen TV over the fireplace flashes on. As well as a three-monitor setup for Dad's desk computer to my left.

The image is shocking and erodes my grief. Mom and Dad are lying unconscious on separate hospital beds. Several white-coated technicians are by their sides, monitoring their vital signs. Nearby, separate IV bags deliver a steady stream of unknown liquid into their veins. I'm certain my parents are at a secure room in Costas's facility.

A spike in Mom's heart rate triggers a high-pitched warning. The skin on my arms pimples and the fine hairs snap up. A male technician rushes to her side. "She's making contact!" He snatches a bottle of serum and a syringe on an accompanying table.

Archer! Mom's voice rips through the home theatre system in front of me. *Listen. We don't have much time.*

The technician is pulling the liquid into the syringe as she speaks. Dad's vital signs surge and another warning bell sends a technician his way. *We're going to be okay, Archer. Listen to your Mother.*

We've been involved in a clandestine government program to project consciousness anywhere in the world, as well as parallel dimensions. We can drop into any location and observe conversations, written material, you name it. Mom's attendant pulls the last bit of serum into her syringe.

I nod and try to process the information.

Through us, the government can monitor any hostile acts planned against the U.S. or its citizens. And we haven't even begun to explore the other dimensions, yet.

Mom's technician removes the syringe from the empty bottle and approaches her IV port. He inserts the needle and presses the plunger.

Your five classmates at Costas' training facility, their parents are involved in this project. Your friends are being held against their will, under threat of violence, to force their parents to come after your father and me. You mustn't let Le Cadavre get you. You're our only hope, you mustn't fall, into their hands.

Mom's voice fades as the sedative overpowers her strong will. But Dad continues where she left off. *When your mother and I agreed to participate in the program, we were aware of the government's commitment for a peaceful use of our psychic abilities.*

I'm totally powerless as the technician removes the syringe from his bottle and empties the sedative in Dad's IV port.

We agreed to being used as psychic spies until…. The drug is having a quicker effect upon Dad. *We agreed to… it. To help. Until we learned, the truth. Beware the Ides of March.* Dad's last words are cryptic.

The image on the television and monitors fades away and I stare at the blank screens. Mom and Dad's funeral was a sham. They're still alive and everything Costas has told me is a lie.

But Dad's mysterious message about the Ides of March, sticks in my mind. This is a vital clue, and I'm sketchy on the details. All that I remember from that period is something about the assassination of Julius Caesar. For some reason, Dad chose not to identify his true message. It could be the other program participants are close to the omniscient state Mom and Dad are in. If the team members are being manipulated by threat of violence against their children, my parents are in imminent danger. Whatever's happening, it's up to me to decipher his meaning.

I take a deep breath and listen to the nighttime symphony of sounds outside our cabin. Thunder rumbles in the distance, and amid the gentle brushing of rose bushes against the windows, I'm reminded how vulnerable I am in the open prairie. The cabin, built in the early '60s, has its own voice of random creaks and pops, too. But I'm jolted back to reality when I hear the front door opening.

Like. Creaking. Open. Heavy footsteps come down the entryway and my heart jumbles into my throat.

A middle-aged man enters the living room. By the looks of him, he lives one block from the *Twilight Zone*. His white hair is stylishly severe, swept back from his broad forehead. He's wearing a baggy pair of black pants with a white dress shirt. The large, black-rimmed glasses on his nose only enhance the sterility of his features.

"So glad to finally meet you, Archer." He smirks, while swinging my door key on his index finger. "Thanks for leaving these. You just made my job easier."

His voice is soft as self-serve ice cream. But the look in his eyes screams, fully loaded, fully cocked, fully fatal, first degree felony.

I assess the situation. Stall for time. "Who in the hell are you?"

"The last person you ever want to meet. But call me Le Cadavre. If you like."

This stranger narrows the distance between us, then removes a boxy looking 9mm Glock from his pants pocket.

I stand up. Take a step toward him. "You just screwed up, Mister."

He nods, as if remembering something. "I've read your

personal file at the facility. I know about your martial arts training. But, my dear, you're out of your league with me."

He points the 9mm toward my face. "I have the gun. You don't. So, turn around. Put your hands behind your back."

I turn around slowly, obediently put my hands in place. When I feel his palm upon my right wrist, I forge a psychic connection and project my consciousness to see through his eyes.

He takes his gun off me in order to handcuff both my wrists. His dominant left hand tucks his automatic in his waistband, while his right clamps around my right wrist. Just as he releases the gun, I twist my body to the right and face him. His eyes open wide, and I knee him in the groin, jerk his wrist around so his arm is locked in place with his right palm face up.

All this happens before he can react, and as he goes down, I brutally force his hand back against his outer forearm until I hear a satisfying snap.

He shrieks like a little girl.

"That's for coming where you're not invited."

He goes for the gun with his good hand and I kick him in the balls again. As he warps into a fetal position, I remove the 9mm from his waistband, pop the magazine out, and eject the chambered bullet.

His anger goes nuclear. His teeth clench together.

I press my foot against his wrist, just to show him who's in control.

"You are so screwed. You don't have any idea who you're dealing with."

"Alright abra cadabra, or whatever you call yourself, you just picked a fight with the wrong person. For starters, you came into our house uninvited. Secondly, you pulled a gun on me."

"To hell with you. You've lost this battle."

"I suppose this is where you say someone's behind me?"

"That's right." He grins. "But let him speak for himself."

"That's the oldest trick in the book." Yet, I glance over my left shoulder. No one's there. My confidence returns and I meet his glare. Until cold, sharp steel kisses my throat.

"Your ass is mine." Costas chuckles. "And if there is a next time, look over both shoulders."

There's no mistaking the satisfaction in his voice. Not even close.

Costas twists toward LC, and the blade nicks the top layer of my skin. "Get up. Get the cuffs on this bitch."

It's almost comical to watch LC try to stand. His right hand is bent unnaturally, and he cradles his balls with his left hand.

"Did I break something down there, abra cadabra?"

He straightens and groans.

The look in his eyes is *The Twilight Zone* meets Freddy Krueger. And Freddy is having a really, really pissy day.

Should I tell him I'm sorry? Probably. But social graces were never my forte.

He pulls a pair of handcuffs out of his pocket with his good hand and reaches between Costas and me to cinch them around my wrists.

"Wow, great dexterity." I laugh. "Bet you'll get a happy face on your next job eval."

Costas jerks me around and slams a fist in my gut. "Shut your mouth, bitch."

I collapse on the couch and gasp for breath. While I struggle to breathe, he cinches my ankles with a plastic zip tie.

"There." Costas backs away, a self-satisfied smirk on his florid, pudgy face. "That should keep you from causing more trouble."

I finally draw a lungful of air as he hands a gun-like device to Le Cadavre.

The refugee from *The Twilight Zone* gives me a grim smile. He holds the weapon up so I can see. "This is a police model Taser, X26."

Costas grins in anticipation.

"It comes with two functions. The first is Drive Stun, which has no other purpose than to cause pain." He leers at me. "A lot of pain." Le Cadavre lifts my T shirt with the tip of the taser, stares at my crescent-shaped birthmark, then places the device against my bare stomach. He pulls the trigger.

Mind-numbing shock explodes across my midsection. I gag and violently twist to break the contact with the Taser. He holds it in place, punishing me with its savage current. The device delivers its devastating voltage and it's more than I can bear.

When the torture finally stops, I collapse against the sofa. Totally spent. Totally beaten. Totally screwed. Tears run down my face as I glare at my tormenter.

"I said you had two functions to look forward to." His eyes blazed like a deranged Charles Manson as he makes an adjustment to the taser. "When I fire the electrodes, you'll lose voluntary control of your muscles. Your sensory nerves and motor nerves will be violently stimulated. Muscle contractions will rack your body."

Le Cadavre looks in my eyes as he points the taser. I search his face for a hint of mercy, but see only dark, animal savagery.

He sights down the tip of the device and I'm reminded of my isolation here.

Our house is too far down the road. Too far from the neighbors. Too far into the wilds.

And no one will hear me scream.

Le Cadavre pulls the trigger.

I am so screwed.

7

FEELING BETTER?

I OPEN MY EYES, ATTEMPT TO swallow, but the inside of my mouth feels like a pile of sun-baked crap. When I try to move, every muscle in my body shrieks in agony. All I can manage is an inch of mobility until I realize leather straps secure my wrists and ankles.

As I lift my head, it's clear I'm strapped on a hospital bed and totally helpless. My room is the size of a large walk-in closet with drab walls and no window. In the corner, above, is a security camera next to a flat-screen TV. I twist my head to look behind me and see a secured metal door with a small, glass opening.

My thoughts ping against the boundaries of my mind—fear on one side and rage on the other. I jerk against my restraints and try to scream. But all I can produce is a ghastly hissing sound. If someone knew I was here, I might have a chance. That someone would be Slash, my boyfriend/classmate of one year. Just two weeks ago, during a psychic training break at Costas' facility, I looked up at Slash over coffee and lost my breath.

His ice-blue eyes sparkle as he smiles. It's not just any smile. The curve of his lips is a visual arc of primal testosterone. When the left corner lifts in a uniquely Slash style, he devastates me with a Hiroshima smile. It's so emotionally nuclear, my heart never stood a chance.

That smile is smooth. It's seductive. It's dangerous.

Smooth like satin sheets. Seductive as forbidden love. Lethal as a razor's edge.

I lean in across the table. Kiss him hard. Taste the sharp edge of my own submission on his lips.

Then, I kiss him again.

He's everything I'm not. He's everything I crave. He's everything I should avoid. With that last thought, I put Slash safely back in his box and acknowledge the memory as a defense mechanism to buffer my feeling of helplessness.

I look around the small room and jerk against my leather restraints. I'm able to work up a bit of saliva and finally speak. "Hello?" Silence looms on the other side of the door. I suspect, whoever is watching, is aware that I'm conscious. Much too soon, it will be time for Costas and his drama.

A gossamer veil finally lifts from my mind and I try to focus on the events that put me here. After Le Cadavre hit me with a double dose of that damned taser, I vaguely remember Costas injecting me with some mind deadening, numb-dumb, drug. Now that I'm awake, there's a strong chance that I'm in a secure part of his facility, probably close to my parents.

That thought comforts me but getting out of here to help them will be nearly impossible. The red light under the closed-circuit camera blinks monotonously and adds to my frustration.

I hear four short beeps outside, and momentarily, the electronic lock retracts and Le Cadavre strolls through the door.

My body tenses. I close my eyes. Clench my teeth. Count on an assault that's sure to come.

Instead, he places a cool, damp cloth across my forehead and gently cleans my face.

I open my eyes and see his concern. He smiles as he tucks a small pillow under my head. "Thought you could use some ice water, too."

He puts the cup against my lips, and I slurp like a fiend, until I'm full. I look up at him as he brushes the hair from my forehead. "Feeling better, now?"

This man is 99.99% pure unadulterated evil, but it's his .01% that has me confused. Several hours ago, he was a raging homicidal maniac and now he's symbolically putting a mint on my pillow as he turns down the bed.

He must have an angle for his actions. So, real or not, I will test his benevolence. I've been tensing my right wrist against the leather restraint, and as I look down, my hand is grayish-blue. "Can you loosen the strap?" I nod submissively toward my wrist, "It's too tight."

I catch a glimpse of the cast on his right wrist as he moves to look. Le Cadavre reaches over with his good hand and loosens the leather belt one notch.

"That better?"

"Yes. Thank you."

He stands to leave, and something flickers across his face. His features go blank and his lips quiver before he says, "Remember your training, Archer."

"What did you say?" I'm stunned.

Le Cadavre's face is now clear and unaffected as he walks over and punches in his door access code. The lock snicks back and he turns toward me. "You're mistaken, my dear. I didn't say anything."

But he did. And it's the exact four words Mom used before I left the house.

8

AS HARMLESS AS
DRINKING WATER

JUST AS LE CADAVRE LEAVES, ALLEN Costas waddles into the room. His immenseness, the pig with a wig, smirks at me, and holds out an empty prescription bottle.

He bends over until his sweaty face is inches from mine. "Have any idea who this prescription is for, Archer?"

His breath has the vile bouquet of raw sewage and I jerk my head away. "Someone your age might have performance issues. Is it your Viagra?"

His face twists with unholy rage and the black hole called Costas pulses with evil. "Bitch, you and your Mother have a smart mouth. The sooner you realize who's in control, the better off you'll be."

Costas shoves the bottle in my face. "Don't deny it, Archer. These were your pills. Ninety doses of Zyprexa. Psychotropic medicine used to treat severe mental illness."

He reaches inside his pocket and removes a diary. "On page 43, you wrote, 'diagnosed with schizophrenia. June 3, 2018.' Your own words, Archer." He throws the journal on my chest.

In a guarded microburst of thought, I engage Mom's training.

"No!" My thoughts race to the speed of light. With

hyper-acuity, I'm aware of what this means. If I'm denied my medicine, there's a rapid cognitive decline, and that's a treacherous path I have no desire to follow.

Compare a normal brain to a 120-volt household circuit. But for the schizophrenic, amp that circuit into a body bruising, brain busting 50,000-volt neural surge. Keep the energy constant for a few days until your mind conjures a continual loop of insane thoughts that somehow appear profound, even spiritual. Once schizophrenia has its claws imbedded in your throat, God releases his hold on your hand and suddenly turns away. His holy light fades to black and you're engulfed with fear—fear of that total and savage darkness.

Terror has a grip on my gut, a hammerlock on my heart, a stranglehold on my sanity. But I'd take the punishing force of Dwayne Johnson or Vin Diesel over this any day, because, with Costas, things always get worse.

"Oh yes." He sneers. "I'm going to take your medicine away. I'm going to drive you insane. After your parents finish the job they started, I'm going to be the last person you ever see alive."

I have to do something.

"Remember my psychic incision class?" He shakes his finger. "The first rule to avoid psychic surveillance?"

I remember clearly, *bury your thoughts so deep that only you can recover them.*

He stares at me. "You were my best student, Archer, and I know what you're thinking. Pity you didn't retain the lessons."

Costas is totally oblivious that I have a scripted plan. I did camouflage my thoughts. He knows only what I want him to know.

My tormentor reaches down and pulls my tee shirt back to expose my stomach. "I have a surprise for you.

Your parents must cooperate to complete my project and your personal safety is my bargaining chip. I'm engaging in brinkmanship with them—your well-being in return for their cooperation. Since I haven't heard from your Mother, I brought something to speed up her decision."

He peels the wrapping from a square medical band aid. "This is a transdermal patch with a powerful, time-released drug. The chemical will enhance your schizophrenic state and produce a profound psychosis within twelve hours. By comparison, this drug makes the effects of LSD seem as harmless as drinking water."

As he leans closer, I jerk against my bindings and thrash my body—anything to keep him from putting the patch on my stomach.

Costas slaps it in place.

His double chin wobbles as he laughs. "Welcome to the next chapter of your sorry life, Archer. You don't cross me and get away with anything."

He slams his fist into my lower abdomen, and I gasp from the blow. Costas raises his hand and gestures to the wall. "Look around, Archer. There's no toilet here. So, if you have to go, you'll lie in your own filth."

He removes a TV remote from his pants pocket. "For your viewing pleasure, I've selected the entire *Three Stooges* collection, to play—backwards."

He presses the start button and my sanity is bombarded with the idiotic antics of Moe, Larry, and Curly. In reverse.

"Welcome to hotel Costas." He struts for the door. "This is the one place you'll never leave."

9

THE BLINKING RED LIGHT

AS THE DOOR CLOSES BEHIND COSTAS, I finally draw a full breath. What is it with this human slug and his anger issues? I take a few shaky breaths and realize the backwards chaos of the *Three Stooges* with its unnatural soundtrack isn't helping my mental equilibrium, either.

But I do have a plan. One in which Le Cadavre plays an unsuspecting part. My right wrist strap wasn't that taut to begin with, however, by restricting the blood flow with pressure against the restraint, it gave the appearance of being too tight.

For whatever bizarre reason, Le Cadavre obliged me by loosening the strap and that may be enough to help me free my hand. Though, there is a small problem of my video surveillance. The all-seeing lens captures my exposed position, spread-eagled and strapped to a metal frame bed. The camera's red-light blinks on, then off. On, then off. On then….

I hold my breath. Wait five seconds. Ten seconds, The red light's still off.

Something or someone, has affected the camera and I don't have time to wonder who. It's time to act, so I tug against my right wrist cuff. It's still plenty snug. I jerk hard and feel leather scrape flesh from the back of my hand.

A quick look up at the camera. Everything's okay. The top of my hand throbs from the abrasion. Try to ignore the pain. Take a deep breath. Put my right shoulder into motion. A transfer of power against the stiff cuff.

Damn it. Still stuck.

Another breath, another heave. My hand moves an inch. Then, one more tug and it's free.

A quick glance at the camera. No blinking light. I jerk my T-shirt up. Rip the patch off. Roll it into a ball. Then fist punch the air in victory. After I tuck the evidence inside my pillowcase, I lift my head. The patch has been in place a few minutes and there's no drug residue I can see on my stomach. Just to be safe, I rub the T-shirt against my skin. Now the patch is gone, I have one less problem.

The red light's still off. Moe, Larry, and Curley are behaving badly. The soundtrack sounds like midgets inhaling helium and squealing like the human pig from *Deliverance*.

There's not much time. I fumble with my right wrist strap. Loosen it one more notch. Now I can get in or out quickly.

Just as I ram my hand back through the restraint, I look up at the camera.

The red-light blinks back on. My heart spurs up my throat and I swallow against the painful beat. I exhale a ragged breath. Is this a bizarre coincidence? Or has Mother's psychic power gotten stronger?

10

BRAIN PAIN

EVEN THOUGH I REMOVED COSTAS' TRANSDERMAL, patch, I've been without my Zyprexa for forty-eight hours. During the last twenty-four, my mind has been strafed with ragged, throbbing pain. The television is still full volume and I haven't slept because my thoughts are out of control. I can't turn them off.

The internal voices started this morning. Soft and seductive. Lilting around the edges. Promising to make things better. If only. If only I'll do it. But I'm not ready to hurt myself. Not yet.

Something flutters across my mind. I try to focus. There's a reason I'm here. For something, or someone? Yes. Someone needs my help.

But who?

A voice shrills. I jerk my head up. Look for the source. The television? Or is it in my mind? I wait and listen. Fearful. Vigilant. Afraid what this new sound might mean.

Through my painful, mental fog, I sense a presence behind me, then hear movement. Men and women with tight, fearful faces move through the door to my bedside.

One woman blanches, puts her hand over her nose.

"My God, Tony, what's that smell?"

Tony puts his arm around her, draws her close. "It's alright, Sue." She avoids looking at me and buries her face in his shoulder.

A shard of lucidity slashes through my mental fog. Shame hits like a spike to the chest. I know what the smell is.

I've been lying in my feces and urine for hours.

Costas moves into sight and I purse my lips. If I had enough saliva, I'd spit on him. Instead, I curl my upper lip. Expose my teeth. "You put the venom in my mind. You're the tabloid brain fucker. The little people warned me. They said fear the false prophet"

Tony lunges at Costas, delivers a glancing blow to his face. "You're an animal. You can't get away with this."

Unfazed, Costas pulls a gun and fires point blank at his chest, then turns it upon Sue. Both are dead before they hit the floor.

The remaining couples rush away from the carnage, screaming and crowding into the corner of the small room. Costas stares them down. "I'll do whatever I want. Look at these two." He gestures with his gun. "Do you want to take their place?"

The nervous cattle won't look at him. Won't make eye contact. They fear the false prophet.

The director points at me. "Your attempts to bring Archer's parents back are pathetic. I don't give a damn how much psychic defense they've put up, unless you defeat them, then your children will take her place. If that doesn't work, I'll kill you all, one by one."

"It's impossible," screams one of the females. "We've tried six times and failed six times."

"Individually, yes." Costas nods, his voice cold as hell. "We've adjusted the dimensional induction compound. Next time, we'll send all eight of you at once. That shouldn't be a problem."

Somewhere, the voice shrieks again. The room goes quiet. Deathly quiet. Tiny O's form on eight mouths. They stare down at me.

My body convulses, my eyes bulge from their sockets, my teeth shred my tongue. In a moment of bloody clarity, I realize that it's me. I'm the one who has been screaming.

Horror ripples across the cattle's faces. Like a vicious wind churning the surface of their darkest fear.

The false prophet gives up a grin. Not just any grin. An apocalypse grin.

My hope hemorrhages and writhes in a death throe. My sanity is in shreds.

I have no hope of escape.

As I lose consciousness, I realize Costas has won.

11

WHEN I COME TO, MY MIND is so amped that I slip back to that place inside. The safe place, where insanity won't follow.

Tucked inside my mental cocoon, waves of calmness soothe my deeper being. I float in a warm embrace, linger for a meter of time amid the flow of comfort. But something moves within me and I know it is time to act. I send a cautious message to another part of my brain.

To listen.

Listen for something.

My first clue is the absence of sound—the backwards soundtrack has stopped.

The room is now empty. I'm totally alone.

Archer?

That tone. So familiar.

Listen to my words. Mother's voice is coming from the television monitor. *Five. The earth is scorched, barren and infected. Nothing lives here, not even hope.*

Four. Above the sterile land, swollen clouds are churning. The promise of deliverance is at hand.

Three. Crystal droplets kiss the parched earth and wash away the horrid presence of affliction.

Something shifts deep inside me.

Two. The cleansing spirituality of that which is good in His sight gathers and penetrates the tainted soil.

One. The power of this holy water reaches where you reside, bathes your soul of darkness and fear. That which was once whole and pure lives again.

My eyes flutter open and I look up at the TV monitor. Mother stares back.

Her face beams with pride. *You didn't forget....*

"My training." I finish the sentence for her.

Mother's mind-clearing technique effectively ends my schizophrenic immersion. Years ago, she always repeated an ancient Japanese teaching during my training. If you're not in a position of power, deceive your foe by becoming what he desires. If he dominates you, show fear. If he wants to break you, appear broken. Then, when the enemy thinks he has won, strike back. Essential in my ruse to deceive Costas was submerging myself in what he wanted me to become, both physically and mentally. To make it work, I had to become absolutely, totally, one-hundred-percent insane. Inside and out.

When Costas produced the Zyprexa and my bogus diary, I knew Mother had planted them in advance, based upon her ability to see future events. To validate Costas' goal, I emulated schizophrenia to mislead him. When Dad told me at the cabin to, 'beware the ides of March,' the details surfaced just moments after my immersion ended. In 44 B.C., a bunch of pissed-off Senators stabbed Julius Caesar in the Theatre of Pompeii, Rome. From that information, I inferred that Costas was planning to use his psychic espionage team to carry out the assassination of the President. Fortunately, my parents refused to cooperate and blocked the dimensional entrance to others who were willing to do Costas' dirty work.

Now that this drama is almost over, I'm ready to attack that fat son of a bitch and bring my parents back, too.

I look up at the camera and its blinking red light.

Mother smiles. *Don't worry, Archer. I fixed it so they'll see a continuous loop of you sleeping.*

My mother is ice-cube-cool.

I slip my right wrist out of the leather restraint and quickly unfasten the other three. When I stand, I step over the bodies and nearly vomit from the blood and carnage. "Don't look, Mom." I slip out of my scrubs and clean myself up. There's a fresh change in the corner, and in moments, I'm ready to rock and roll.

Mom's face twists with concern. *I can control the electronic locks and most of the personnel on the way to central control. That's where they're holding your father and me.*

"What about the video monitors on the way there?"

It's all right if I don't spread myself too thin. I'll handle the cameras and anyone you meet on the way. Best case scenario, it could get dicey if you run in to more than five people.

Dicey is not want I want to hear. But what choice is there? Three lives depend on my actions. I plan to get us out alive.

Mom watches me as I move to the door. When my hand touches the knob, she triggers the electronic lock and it snicks back. I step into the corridor and her image flashes onto the hallway monitor screen. She motions me to keep walking.

The floor is sticky against my bare feet and I don't want to know what it's from. It's like nipply cold in here, until I realize that my scrubs are paper thin. I look up at the monitor and Mom puts a warning finger against her lips. *Shh. Two men are coming your way. Don't say anything or make eye contact. Above all, don't bump into them.*

Great. Is this what she meant when she said dicey? Two

bulky security guards, built as solid as manhole covers, enter the walkway and amble into sight side by side. It appears that they're committing umpteen-thousand-pounds of combined body mass into a wide, hallway sweeper.

They move toward me, controlled by Mother, mindless of my presence. Three feet separates the nearest man's shoulder from mine. Two feet and it doesn't look good. It's one foot, now, and closing. He's going to hit me.

My body is flush with the wall, my arms frozen by my side, my heart flutters in my chest.

He's inches away.

With no place to hide, I will my body to melt into the wall. Will away every inch of exposed flesh. Will myself into a size zero.

It's going to be close, so I suck it up, suck it up, suck it up.

But it isn't enough.

At the last moment, he leans into his buddy, says something. Almost hits my shoulder as my hand brushes his gun belt.

They pass me by and don't suspect a thing.

I glance at their backs. Taste the sweat on my upper lip. Finally, I remember to breathe.

Now that was dicey.

12

SIXTY SECONDS TILL ETERNITY

I WATCH THE TWO GOONS WALK away and relax when Mother's image springs back on the flatscreen.

She winks and nods. *Continue down this hallway until you come to a dead end. Turn right and stop outside the double doors.*

Within minutes, I'm in front of the central control entrance, peering through the door's window. Directly in front of me, Mom and Dad lie on separate hospital beds, unconscious and oblivious to the activity around them. Inside the spacious room, six white-coated technicians are on the floor, two of which tend to my parents and an additional one who monitors the security console. That makes seven people. Two more than Mom can control. I hope to God she can handle them.

A closed-circuit television screen is just above the security console, and when Mom's image flashes on, that is my cue to enter. The door's electronic lock retracts, and I push my way inside.

No one notices me at first. People move and talk, check charts and go about their duties. One technician looks my way, raises his hand, but before he can sound an alarm, the man's body movements cease, his arms go limp. The worker's face still reflects alarm over my presence before Mom took over. A pregnant hush fills the room as the other attendants freeze in place.

I don't have a good feeling about this, but I won't let my nerves take over. So, I weave around the technicians, careful not to touch them or look in their eyes.

Mom maintains control of the room, and I plant myself next to her bed. But a jerky movement from the corner of my eye startles me. A lone technician moves toward me like a marionette. His awkward movements show his attempt to fight against Mother's mental control.

A quick glance at the flat screen. Mother's demeanor says that she can handle this. Reassured, I notice the tray in the man's hands. It holds two ampoules of amber liquid and a couple of syringes.

Archer, I had him compound the drug that will awaken us from our dimensional induction trance. Empty one vial in each of our IV ports.

The puppet stops in front of me and his harsh breath washes across my face. He fights against mom's control—spittle flies from his mouth and runs down his lower lip. His eyes jerk from side to side and I avoid looking at him when I pick up a vial and one syringe.

I remove the syringe's protective wrapper, pop the cap off and insert the needle in the bottle's rubber stopper. Then I turn it up, pull the plunger back and fill the syringe. In the back of my mind, I listen to the steady electronic heartbeats coming from my parents' vital sign monitors.

Within a few minutes, I deliver both doses into their bloodstream. Mother's image is still on the CCTV monitor and the immobile technicians are as frozen as Mount Rushmore. Still, something bothers me.

My feeling of dread surges when the man who brought the vials, jerks and drops his tray. The empty glass ampoules shatter on the floor. A nearby worker twists around to face me. His companion, at Dad's side, also begins to move.

I scan the room and see the emerging scowls on several faces. And then I hear a door crash open. Le Cadavre rushes in, past the security console, with three armed thugs behind him.

"Mom," I plead, "I need some help. *Now.*"

A quick look at the monitor stuns me to the core. What the hell is going on? Mom's face is now lifeless. Her mouth slack. Yet, there is a glimmer of recognition in her eyes. I know she can still hear me.

Le Cadavre approaches with impunity. Glares at me. Rumbles with laughter. "You see, Archer, your mother isn't the only one with psychic ability. I knew what she was planning before she had the technician make the compound. So, I switched her wake-up drug with a recipe of my own. A batch of nasty chemicals that brings death in minutes." He glances at his watch. "By the looks of it, it's sixty seconds till eternity."

I square off with him. "You're lying."

"If I am," he spreads his hands, "why can't your mother control me?"

I scan the room and my heart lurches up my throat. The once immobile technicians begin to circle around me. Some jerk like zombies, others are more coordinated.

Le Cadavre cups his hand behind one large ear. "Listen, what's that sound?"

What the hell is he talking about? I look around, frantic to understand. Then, I hear it. The unmistakable sound of my parent's telemetry. The frantic pinging of two vital sign monitors. It is the signal of impending death. My parents' hearts are beating way too fast.

I glance at Mom's monitor. Her pulse registers one hundred-forty-five. Dad's is over one-fifty. Both are climbing.

The two machines emit a warning signal.

Le Cadavre grins. "How does it feel, Archer, knowing that your parents are alive, after a staged death, only to be killed by you?"

I don't have time to think. I'm surrounded by eleven men. Like a lone kid, circled by thugs, I face off with insurmountable odds. It's me against them.

"Feel all alone, Archer?" He smirks. "Such a pity. But know when your parents are dead, there'll be someone you can lean on, and that's me."

I have no idea what he is talking about. My focus is on my parents. Mom's television image draws my attention. There is something strange in her eyes.

I look back at Le Cadavre. "What the hell are you talking about, asshole?"

He taps his watch. "Thirty seconds, Archer. Don't interrupt me, because I have some news for you." He points to Mother's monitor image. "Just keep your eyes on her."

All I can focus on is the raging rhythm of my parents' heartbeats.

Le Cadavre smirks. "In the summer of 1994, your Mother was raped on her way home in a vacant house just blocks from her apartment. No police were involved, and your Father never learned about it. It was your Mother's little secret. A secret that grew into a baby girl she carried for nine months. She prayed that the child was your Father's, but in her heart she knew better."

Raw fear twists Mom's face.

My mouth goes dry. My heart hammers a hole in my chest. Something sick and evil squirms in my gut.

Mom's eyes are alive with fear. Fear generated by truth.

"Fifteen seconds and counting Archer."

The vital signs warning shrills again. My pulse throbs in my temple. "You're making this shit up."

"Could be, but the proof is in the pudding." He lifts his shirt to expose a small, tan birthmark, in the shape of a crescent.

My throat closes shut, barely stifles my scream.

"Ever see this, Archer? You have one in the same place. I saw it before I tazed you at the ranch house. Then I remembered that night when I raped your mother."

My hands tremble as I slowly lift my scrub top. I glance down. There is an identical mark. Just like his.

"This can't be true." But when I look in Mother's eyes, I know it is.

Le Cadavre sees it, too.

Both monitors shriek a final, fatal warning. Mother and Father flatline. Utter terror bears its fangs, rips my heart, slices my sanity, and claims my soul.

In the space of five minutes, I realize three things. We can't escape, I have killed both my parents, and the monster called Le Cadavre is my real father!

He holds his arms out. "You're not alone while I'm here, Archer." My father puckers his lips and beacons me closer. "Come give Daddy a kiss."

13

THE ROAD TO RUIN

TEN MINUTES LATER, LE CADAVRE SHOVES me in another holding cell and I stumble into Slash's heavily tattooed arms. My boyfriend Slash is my antiestablishment rogue male. His honey-blond hair falls across his eyes and when I look up at him, his lip labret sparkles with a surgical sheen from the overhead lights. I hold him tight. Bury my head against his chest and let the tears flow. He embraces my suffering as I soak his Nirvana tee with my pain and anguish.

He strokes my hair. "Le Cadavre made sure all of us saw what happened. What you did with your parents."

'All of us' meaning my five classmates at the facility. And 'what you did' meaning that I lethally injected Mom and Dad.

Grief hikes out of a dark hole and spikes my heart. "I killed them, Slash."

He tenses protectively, draws me closer. Slash nestles his lips against my ear, and I smell pot on his breath. "You were set up Arch. Le Cadavre switched the drug that should have ended your parent's trance. It wasn't your fault."

"It's true, but you didn't inject the drug. I did. I pushed the plunger. I ended their lives."

Slash absorbs my pain. Lifts his sunglasses. Releases me and takes a deep breath. He pushes his disobedient hair back and pulls a small flask from his pocket. Unscrews the cap and takes a long pull. Slash winks and makes air quotes with his forefingers. "You know Arch, rum may be the road to ruin, but at least it's the scenic path. So, wet your lips. Have a taste."

I so need this distraction. Swept up in his aura of recklessness, I take a long pull. Feel the burn. Try not to think of my parents. But a guilty dose of reality hits me as I look into his ice-blue eyes. Men can either compliment your life or complicate it. Slash does both.

I know it's a given. I'm a moth, he's the flame. But why I keep flying into the fire confounds the devil out of me. Slash is everything I should avoid. Until chemistry 101 kicks in. Then old-fashioned need, or just plain old lust, spreads its velvet wings and screams, 'Houston, we have lift off.' The rest is history.

I lay my head back on his chest, and wonder, how am I going to live without my parents?

14

SLASH NUZZLES MY EAR, DRAPES HIS arm over my shoulder, and guides me toward a door opposite the one I came in. He turns the knob and quickly ushers me inside a larger room. My other four classmates turn and stare at me with horror-filled eyes. Behind them is a closed-circuit television flashing a continual loop. The loop of me injecting my parents with the death-inducing drug. The coda to this creep show shows Mom and Dad flatlining.

"Turn that shit down," Slash yells. Jacqui Chen quickly complies. Then my friends rush over and smother me in a collective hug.

Twenty-one-year-old Luanne Martinez shouts, "You were set up, Archer."

The slightly older, Perry Silverman, doesn't miss a beat, "Le Cadavre killed them. It wasn't your fault."

A short, round, adolescent, with bright pink cheeks, wraps his arms around my torso and squeezes until I nearly cry from the love.

Mark Sand looks up at me and it takes my breath away. There is nothing like the smile of a person with Down's Syndrome, especially when he loves you. His eyes ooze soulful innocence and total acceptance, but it is the dose of mischief that really squeezes my heart. I adore this tiny, pink-cheeked person, and I know he loves me, too.

He looks down. "Mark Sand saw whatcha did, Archer." The endearing reference to himself, always in third person, brings a smile to my face. At this point, I need every grin I can get.

He hugs me again and glances back at the television screen. His face crinkles up in pain. Tears well up in his eyes as my parents' monitors flatline. Guilt twists my gut, because the couple Costas killed, Sue and Tony, were Mark Sand's parents.

"Archer, Mark Sand has a feeling."

This dear young orphan tucks his head close to my chest. He sniffles softly. "We're not in Kansas anymore."

No other comment can crystallize the situation we're in.

I look into my friends' faces and see the somber questions there. They've always turned to me for direction. Leadership. I hope that no one else dies under my command.

"All right, guys," I whisper. "Get in a circle, hold hands, and make sure your palms touch. I've got a plan."

The circle forms quickly and each palm touches the other. I glance at the camera in the corner and know we are taking a chance. There are only a few minutes to pull this off.

"I'd like a moment of silence for my parents." Heads go down and Mark Sand sniffles.

For all appearances, we are honoring the dead, but appearances aren't always truthful. I'm using a minor chakra, a psychic energy pathway, located in the palm of each friend's hand to connect mentally with them and relate the events over the past few days. It is a technique Mother taught me and one I passed along to my five class-mates between training classes.

Costas never mentioned this device in class, but if he's

watching, he might recognize the technique. So, I urgently pass the images, rapid fire, filling my friend's minds with everything that happened since my meeting with Costas three days ago. Everything, except the senseless murder of Mark Sand's parents.

My heart is embalmed with grief over my parents' deaths, but I can't focus on that now. A burst of righteous anger cleaves my chest as I form the images that will deliver us from evil and avenge four murdered people. I mentally convey how we're going to kick Costas's ass, when we're going to do it, and where it's going to happen.

We will do it in the next five minutes.

15

YOUR SOUL FOR A PORSCHE

WHEN THE DOOR CRASHES OPEN, SLASH pulls me to his side and my friends gather protectively around me. Costas and Le Cadavre strut through like the triumphal Caesar and entourage returning to Rome. Only, I can't imagine Caesar having a pig snout nose like Costas. I don't see Caesar being able to smell buried truffles at three hundred feet, either. In the next few minutes, however, Costas will have a multilayered job resume touting truffle hunter and former espionage director because I intend to change his employment status drastically.

Right on cue, Mark Sand moves in front of me and gets in Costas' face. "Let us go right now. And Mark Sand will act like this never happened. But if you don't let us go, Mark Sand will dig out the hole you're hiding in, and Mark Sand will kill you. Then Mark Sand will whistle as he shovels dirt in your face."

"The retard's a comedian." Le Cadavre crosses his arms.

"Mark Sand will tell you one time. One time only. Don't ever use the "R" word." The adolescent with Down's Syndrome points his forefinger like an imaginary gun at Le Cadavre's forehead. "Go ahead. Make me do it."

Le Cadavre rolls his eyes. "Whatever."

With everyone's attention on Mark Sand, I discretely move my hand to the back of my scrubs and reach inside for the gun. The small .38 caliber revolver I lifted off the armed guard in the hallway outside of my cell. But, just as my fingertips touch the handle, my wrist is violently jerked upward, and Slash grabs the gun instead. He removes it and jams its cold muzzle against my left temple.

What the hell? This isn't part of the plan. My fellow classmates jerk in horror, some put their hands up as they recoil. But it's the expression on Slash's face, that look of smugness, of ultimate triumph, that stomps the life out of my heart and soul. The one person I unconditionally trust has turned on me.

With feral cunning, Slash gives me a crooked little grin. First, it was the death of my parents, now, this brutal betrayal.

Costas takes the gun from Slash and slaps a set of car keys in Slash's palm. "Enjoy the Porsche, son, you've earned it."

I shake my fist in the air. "My parents are dead, Costas is planning to kill the President, and you sold us out for a car?" I gasp for air and step back from Slash. The amused look on his face does an acid etch upon my heart.

"Arch, it's not just a car. It's a Porsche 911. Targa. Secondly, Costas has no plans to kill the President. When you psychically downloaded the events from the past three days, you misinterpreted your father's message. His reference to the Ides of March did involve Caesar and the Senators who turned on him. But Caesar was a metaphor for the death of our country, the good old U.S.A. And the Senators obviously represent Costas and company. Costas has no plans to kill the President, rather, with my help, we'll loot the country's secrets and sell them to the highest bidder."

Slash reaches out to brush my hair back, and I slap him hard. Freaking hard. "How dare you touch me. You betrayed me!"

He rubs his cheek, continues like nothing has happened, "It seems that after your parent's death, the rest of the team learned the project's true objective, and no one had the stomach for the job. Except me. So, I cut a deal when I learned what Costas was driving. My soul for a Porsche? Hell yes. And when we sell America's covert secrets, I get one-third off the top. After a few days of psychic espionage, I'll never have to work again. It's too bad you couldn't be a part of this, Arch. But I realize you have standards, and know you'd never agree to it. Fortunately, for Costas, I don't have that kind of baggage. In your perfect world, bad things shouldn't happen to good people. But this isn't a perfect world, and, if I had to do it again, I'd still sell out for the money."

Costas has the gun on me, and he breaks out in a shit-eating grin. Then nods at Le Cadavre. "Take this bitch and her friends to the church. Fire up your transistor radio and make damn sure you start with Archer. After that, take out her classmates. I'll finish the loose ends here, and when the money hits the offshore account, we'll disappear."

Le Cadavre licks his lips and moves toward me with his handcuffs. "I'm looking forward to a little Father/Daughter time, Archer. I'll do my best not to disappoint you."

16

TAKE A DEEP BREATH

UNSEEN HANDS FLIPPED A SWITCH INSIDE the gutted country church and cleaved the shadows with a joyless shaft of brilliance.

Le Cadavre stepped into the light, took a deep breath, and felt the sordid fabric of darkness surge within him. He was moved by the desecration he had inflicted upon this holy structure. No amount of God's presence remained. Nor would anything alter the impending violence to come.

He had chained Archer to a medical dissection table where the pulpit had once stood. With her bare flesh exposed to the cool air, the fine hairs on her forearms stood on end. Her thighs and torso were pimpled from the cold, stainless-steel beneath her back. She drew rapid breaths through her mouth as shivers erupted from within her torso.

"Welcome to my sanctuary." Le Cadavre removed his shirt and stepped closer to Archer. "I hope you're ready to play."

I TRY TO QUIET MYSELF. TAKE a deep breath. But the calmness aborts when Le Cadavre begins to remove his crisp white dress shirt.

Two black leather straps drape over each bare shoulder and extend halfway down his chest. In turn, a circular band connects them, front and back, to form a short harness. A small transistor radio is held in the middle by the parallel straps.

In contrast to my breathing, his is slow and methodical. With rising dread, I watch him insert a nipple ring on his left side. He casually clips a bare, nine-inch wire to the silver ring and forms a crude antenna with an adapter on its other end.

His eyes are cold and flat, like a fanged predator. I refuse to beg for mercy, and I have no doubt that I and my four classmates will be killed. But it's better for him to spend his time on me, than my friends. At least I can buy them a reprieve before the inevitable happens. One hour, maybe two, that's all I can hope for.

Le Cadavre connects the adapter to his transistor radio and completes the antenna. Then he turns to say, "Two days ago when I searched your house, I couldn't find your psychic imprint. It still puzzles me."

I shift against my restraints, aware that I'm completely nude and unable to cover myself. His eyes flicker in the cold, overhead light and he sniffs the air twice.

"Even now, I can't pick up any memory of your personal or psychic trauma. That bothers me deeply. It's never happened before."

My mouth is dry. I lick my lips. "For some psychics, it's difficult to connect with those related to them. You say I'm your daughter, so that could be the case."

Le Cadavre looks thoughtful as he touches the birthmark on his torso. "That may be true, or it could be nothing. Since we're in a sharing mood, I want to tell you that

Costas ordered your parents' death. When we couldn't persuade them to spy for us after we kidnapped you, they left us little choice. Thanks to you, you did our dirty work by killing them. After their deaths, the other team members found Jesus and refused to cooperate, but your dear Slash took the initiative and is stealing America's secrets as we speak. If you do have a hidden flaw, it would be your choice of men."

I bite my lip hard. Taste the blood.

A calculated beat ensues. "I think our Father/Daughter sharing is about over. Emotional bonding is vastly overrated." He rubs his hands together. "It's time I introduced you to some of my friends. The voices."

Le Cadavre thumbs his radio on and tunes to a station. "I want you to meet Brother Hell, a Pentecostal minister."

When your very soul hangs in the balance, do you want to spend an eternity in Hell? The minister's words and inflection are the strident voice of extremist religion. Religion meant to beat the weak-willed into obedience and submission. A tent revival on steroids.

Momentarily, Le Cadavre moves the dial to another station. "This one," he says, "is a rabid financial commentator."

The economy will be devastated after the next election. Chaos will reign, terror will cripple our country, and people will riot in the streets.

He moves the knob slightly. "A little trick I learned is to put the dial between two stations and get bleedover from both programs as they fade in and out. The brilliant part is that the words will offer direction to our encounter. So, I hope you'll enjoy our intimate evening together."

Le Cadavre removes a black velvet pouch from his pocket and lays it on my bare stomach. He spreads it open to reveal four surgical steel scalpels inside. With an air of reverence, he removes one and holds it up to the light. The deadly blade sparkles along the length of its razor-sharp edge.

The radio transmission kicks back in and Brother Hell returns. *If your foot causes you to stumble, I say cut it off!*

My torturer steadies the scalpel. Presses the blade against my right ankle and makes the incision.

I shriek in pain and horror. My desperate cry batters the walls of this desecrated church and echoes in the darkness. Darkness that mocks me with indifference.

THE RADIO CRACKLES AND THE FINANCIAL wannabe cuts in, *If you fear the coming economic crisis, then stop what you're doing right now. Stop and listen....*

Le Cadavre abandoned his incision and smiled before he licked Archer's warm blood off his hand. A moment later, he grinned. "So vibrant. Your essence is of mine, daughter, strong and deep. My bond with you will live forever."

Brother Hell emerged from the vapors of the radio static with a second message. *If thy hand offends thee, cut it off. It is better for thee to enter into life maimed, then having two hands to go into hell, into the fire that shall never be quenched....*

Le Cadavre moved up to Archer's right hand and readied his scalpel. He placed the honed edge against her skin, poised over her wrist. The radio was mute, until the financial commentator returned. *My message about the coming crisis is simple—you have five actions to consider. Take the first, which is apparent as the little finger on your hand.*

"This shouldn't hurt at all." Le Cadavre chuckled softly as he sliced Archer's smallest finger off. "Well, maybe just a little."

I PROMISED MYSELF THAT I WOULDN'T beg, but crushing pain explodes up my arm. "Stop! I'll give you all my money, whatever you want. Just please, please stop. I haven't done anything to you. I'm your daughter, doesn't that mean anything? Just let us go. I'll never tell."

"You haven't done anything to me?" Le Cadavre leans closer. Slams his wrist cast into my face. "What do you call this? I call it a broken wrist. And what do you call the blood I've been pissing for two days? Daughter or not, I don't owe you anything."

My cries hiccup in my throat as blood shoots from my hand and pools along my bare thigh.

I'm all alone. In a violated church. At the mercy of a monster who is my father. The same bastard who tricked me into killing my parents. As the last bitter truth rapes what's left of my hope, I know I'm going to die.

THE RADIO SPUTTERED TO LIFE, AND Brother Hell cleared his throat. *And if thine eye offend thee, pluck it out, and cast it from thee, it is better for thee to enter into life with one eye, rather than having two eyes to be cast into hellfire.*

Le Cadavre raised his arms and a fine sheen of Archer's blood coated his cast. "Daughter," he whispered, "the moment of truth is upon us. I am here to serve the voices. Voices that direct me with their divine will."

A moment of static, then the financial guru returned. *I have given you the five options for economic survival. In the coming financial apocalypse, there will be two investors. The fool and the wise man. The fool will be shortsighted and indiscriminate in his investment strategy. He will be slaughtered, financially. Yet, the wise man will contemplate his actions and reap benefit from the turmoil in the marketplace. The clever investor will use his God given intelligence to gather the profits during the upheaval. Everything before him will be for the taking, for him and him only. So, heed my advice, bleed profit from every opportunity. Don't hesitate in your actions. Don't second guess. Don't settle for less. Take the bounty before you. Take it all and leave the bones behind.*

Le Cadavre held the scalpel over Archer's chest, his body trembling. He was eager to plunge naked steel into her flesh, but he wavered in his delivery. For the moment, there was a more important agenda than killing her.

I CLOSE MY EYES, TENSE MY body, prepare for the blow. Then, a door crashes open. "Stop," someone screams, and I open my eyes. Le Cadavre poises above me, his face twisted with anger. "I had a plan for you, Archer. You weren't going to die until I got what I wanted. But, if I can't have you, then no one will." He jerks the scalpel up, then lunges down. The surgical instrument drives toward my chest and I'm a heartbeat away from death.

A gunshot violates the church and its muzzle flash slashes the darkness around us. Le Cadavre drops the scalpel, falls to the floor, and jerks with bastard rhythm. He clutches vainly at his gushing chest wound and then goes still.

The slap of running feet echoes in the church, but I can't see past the light around me, until a face appears above me. It's Slash, and he is both pissed as hell and relieved.

"Arch, Arch, *Arch,*" he repeats like a mantra as he un-

fastens my bindings. He kisses my forehead and cheeks repeatedly as I sit up. Like a true gentleman, he hands me Le
Cadavre's shirt.

I take stock of my injuries—a superficial cut on the
right ankle. And my missing finger is—well, still missing.

Slash pats down Le Cadavre's pockets, pulls out a clean
handkerchief and expertly binds my wound.

I hold my bloody hand up, and cry against his shoulder.
"With nine fingers, I can't play classical piano worth a crap.
But, there's always the harmonica."

As I back away to look at him, his expression is priceless.

I touch his face gently. "Thanks to you, I can't com-
plain. I'm still alive."

He brushes my hair back and this time I don't slap him.

"I thought you'd sold out for the money, Slash."

"I may be irresponsible and a sloth boy, but I love you
Arch, and would never betray you. I had a plan after you
injected your parents, so I approached Costas. He told me
about the psychic spying. Said none of the team would do
it. I accepted and Costas took the bait. I knew he intended
to kill you and our classmates, and I figured he'd farm out
the dirty work to Le Cadavre. It was just a matter of timing,
to neutralize Costas and get to you in time."

"How did you find us? This church is really remote."

"I overheard a conversation between Costas and Le Cadavre after you were brought from central control."

"How did you get away?" I touch his arm.

"Simple, after Le Cadavre left with you guys, I told
Costas that I needed to go pee."

"And then?"

"You know me. Since they don't allow cell phones in
the facility, I've always smuggled one in and hidden it in
the restroom waste basket, the same place where I put my
pot. After that, I called 911."

"Did they get Costas?"

Slash's face darkens with rage. "No! When the police came, they searched the entire facility and he was gone. Arch, it's like he knew. Knew it was going to happen. He just disappeared."

In the sudden quiet, we both focus on the pool of blood around Le Cadavre.

"I had to shoot him. He was going to kill you if I didn't."

"I'm damned glad you did." But then something sparks within me. I slip off the steel table and step over to Le Cadavre's body—moisten my forefinger with saliva, bend down, press it against his birthmark, and rub. The small mark disappears, and I breathe a sigh of relief.

"What's that about, Arch?"

I'm not ready to share this information with anyone—Le Cadavre lied about being my father. I just shrug, "Tying up loose ends, lover boy. Let's get our classmates out of their cells and go see the police."

"The sooner the better. This place creeps me out."

Slash's cell phone suddenly pings with a video message. He looks at me and hesitates.

I have an intuitive rush, and shudder. "Better open it."

He removes it from his pocket, turns the speaker phone on, and moves the screen so I can see.

It's Costas.

The director grins. *"Archer, I'm sure you're still alive to hear this, so I'll make it quick. You and I still have unfinished business. Don't even try to find me, because I'll be off the grid until I come after you. Even though your parents aren't around to help you anymore, I'm sure they'd agree, when you play with the big dogs, someone always gets hurt."*

The screen goes blank and I take a shaky breath. "How the hell did he know you rescued me? It seems like he's always one step ahead of us."

Slash shakes his head. "He's one slippery eel."

"Let's get the hell out of here, Slash. Then we'll find Costas, fire up the stove, and fricassee his nuts."

17

WELCOME HOME

SOMETHING MOVED WITHIN THE DARKNESS OF the church, and a quiet padding of feet brought the man into the shaft of brilliance. Kneeling next to Le Cadavre, who lay on the cold floor in a pool of blood, he gently rolled the body over and placed two fingers against the carotid artery. Surprisingly, there was a pulse. With a sharp slap to the face, he roused Le Cadavre to consciousness.

Frothy blood bubbled across Le Cadavre's lips and the man gently wiped it away. His teacher was dying, and time was slipping away. He needed Le Cadavre's guidance, he needed direction. And he needed it now.

As if sensing the question, Le Cadavre revived just enough to address his student, "Go after Archer. If you need help, initiate Doctor Navarro. He has the darkness, and still fights it. If you can't turn him, harvest him like the others."

The gunshot victim coughed, and crimson flowed across his lips. "There's a pill in my pocket. Get the induction equipment, too." The man opened a black bag he'd brought, removed the facility's equipment, and placed the sunglasses and headphones on his mentor's eyes and ears. He hit the power switch and gave his guru the pill. Le Cadavre coughed more blood. "You have direction now, finish what I've started."

The chest wound bubbled fresh blood and the student knew that death was near. He reluctantly lowered his mentor's head and faced his own reflection in the life-blood on the floor.

His face was featureless, muted by a thick layer of flesh-colored body paint. He had no eyebrows or eyelashes or even hair. Just three years ago, Le Cadavre had turned him and created his new persona. Father Muerte. Father Death was an apt name for an emotionless killer, one who craved chaos, death, and destruction more than any student Le Cadavre had seen. There was a special need for Archer and the knowledge she carried. Knowledge she was unaware of. Knowledge crucial to Costas and Le Cadavre's plan.

Father Muerte would help Costas exploit it, then would kill Archer and all those on her family tree.

Or, he would die trying.

He rose from his master's side, picked up a five-gallon can of paint solvent in the corner, splashed the liquid around the room. Then left a trail behind him and set the can down when he reached the door. A flick of a match set the church ablaze as he closed the door on this chapter of his life. He had no doubt that Le Cadavre would be dead before the flames reached him.

LE CADAVRE LAID HIS HEAD AGAINST the floor and felt the flames creep toward him. Within a minute, the super-heated air melted his hair. Then his pants began to smolder from the encroaching fire. He jerked into a fetal position and rolled away from the crackling inferno.

He had come full circle as he lay upon the floor of his gutted country church, a church that he'd delivered unto darkness so thick, so total, Satan would have wept for joy.

It was a place where he'd ignored the stench of spilled blood. Ignored desperate pleas. Ignored his victim's screams.

It was a place of cruelty and darkness. A place the devil called home.

Seconds before the flames reached him, he looked over the edge of the sunglasses and thought he saw a figure moving through the fire. Something or someone, tall and powerful, wavered before him. As the wooden structure crackled around him, the fire began feeding upon Le Cadavre's exposed flesh.

Moments before the immersion kicked in, he heard the figure utter two words, "Welcome Home."

And the roaring flames surged as the devil ignored his victim's screams.

18

DOWN THE RABBIT HOLE

IT IS MIDMORNING, AND SLASH AND I are having mochas at the local Starbucks where we gaze at each other over our drinks. He glances away and I sense he has something on his mind. In the pregnant silence, my thoughts revisit the last two weeks since I killed my parents. The guilt over what I did is as palpable as their missing presence. But the hardest part of this ordeal was telling Mark Sand that *his* parents were dead. My young friend was devastated and broke down in tears. "Where will Mark Sand go, Archer? What will Mark Sand do?"

Slash returns his gaze to me, and my sad thoughts return to the present. I can tell by the excitement in his eyes he has something important to share.

He reaches out, takes my good hand in his. "Archer, what if I told you I have a way to find Costas. Would you go after him?"

I remember the heart-crushing effect of watching my parents' flat-line. "Hell yes." I slam the table with my good fist. "In a heartbeat. Anything to put Costas' nuts in a grinder."

Slash gives me a lopsided grin and I lean closer. "Tell me how."

"After I called the police, Costas high-tailed it out of the building. In all the confusion, I did a look see in the big man's office." He reaches in his shirt pocket and holds up two pill bottles. "Here are a few of the things I found. These are the dimensional induction drugs. One is for a thirty-minute immersion. The other is permanent. Also, here's the dimensional induction device you got from Doctor Navarro. Costas explained that the pills only put the user in a receptive state to start an induction. The sunglasses and headphones deliver the right frequency visually and auditorily to allow travel. When Costas thought I was going to spy for him, he said the drug and headset allows the user to psychically 'drop in' to any location in the real world, as well as alternate dimensions."

I pick up the larger vial and study the label. Inside, are six tablets that allow a thirty-minute trip. The second bottle has a single pill. "This one is for an indefinite time?"

He gives a solemn nod.

"Any idea how the drug and headset work?"

"It didn't come with a manual, so the answer is no."

I shrug. Swirl my cup. Take a sip of mocha. "I think it's a good day for a trip down the rabbit hole."

"It could be dangerous." Slash turns my hand over, pretends to study it.

"That didn't stop Alice."

"This isn't a fairy tale, Arch. There's a good chance you could get hurt. We don't know how the drug works or where your consciousness goes once it takes effect. It's a total shot in the dark."

"Mom and Dad took that risk and lived." I look down at the table to hide my tears. "They lived just long enough for me to kill them."

I look up at Slash. Emotion diffuses his eye color. Color that turns to an angry hue. He leans in, just inches from my face. "Fucking stop. Focus on finding Costas. *He* killed your parents. You didn't."

He's right. I've got to come to terms with what I did. And it is going to take time. But truth is, Slash is behind me. Totally. I give his hand a squeeze. "I'll freakin' claw my way down the rabbit hole if it leads us to Costas."

19

WELCOME TO ELSEWHERE

I SIT DOWN ON SLASH'S COUCH, kick off my shoes, and settle on the pillow he's placed for my head. While I make myself comfortable, my eyes search his face and my brain registers his five-alarm fear. Fear that ratchets up my anxiety. There is sweat on Slash's brow as he reluctantly takes a pill from the vial.

He hands me the tablet. "Costas said to put it under the tongue, and it'll activate in a few minutes."

"Is there any downside, or side-effect from the pill?"

"Costas told me your parents were the first to do the permanent immersion pill. The couple he sent to subdue your parents tried the new dimensional induction compound, which lasted only ten minutes. No one's done the half-hour pill, so you're the first." Slash looks up at the living room clock. "It's almost noon, so let's get started."

I put Dr. Navarro's sunglasses and headphones on and thumb the power switch. The LED lights on the inside of the glasses begin to flash randomly, and a chaotic sound emanates from the headset. When the tablet is in place, I feel a tingling sensation, almost like the fizz of a carbonated drink. I try not to think about the danger of what I am doing and move my attention to the rush of Saturday morning traffic filtering through the apartment walls. Somewhere down the street, children's voices rise above the din.

I peer over the edge of the sunglasses—the wall clock shows one-minute past noon.

Then two.

It drags to three.

I begin to wonder if this will work.

Four minutes tick by.

Change to five.

After ten minutes, I give up.

I'm a fool. A fool to try to find Costas. A fool to hope I could avenge my parents' deaths. And, like a mortal wound, my hope bleeds away, until all that is left is the worthless husk of a fool without hope.

Tears trickle down my face as I stand. But, when I glance around, I'm no longer in Slash's apartment, I'm in a crowded hospital foyer, inside another woman's mind. I see through her eyes. See the people around us, hear their anxious chatter, smell the closeness of sweating bodies.

I watch as she pulls a tissue from her purse to dry her tears. Then she glances at a wall mirror between the elevators to check her mascara. She looks at her reflection, and I glimpse a weathered version of myself with light streaks of gray hair and a few extra pounds. But there is no question. It's another me. Another Archer. Archer 1.

ARCHER 1 PUT THE KLEENEX AWAY as heat rose into her cheeks. Her mind screamed at the damn elevators, God, what is the delay!

The phone call from ten minutes ago confirmed her worst fear. Father's COPD had worsened, and he had been moved from the hospital's cardiac unit to the hospice upstairs. The nurse had been kind. "Your Father's in a coma, and you should get here as soon as possible."

I'M TUCKED INSIDE ARCHER 1'S MIND, and her Father—my Father in an alternate dimension—is dying. Her thoughts batter me with the force of a raging tsunami.

THERE WAS SO MUCH ARCHER 1 needed to say to Father, so much unsaid for too many years. A hard little knot formed in her throat, and she trembled, trying to keep back the fear. But anger clenched her fists.

Her earliest memories were trying to earn Father's affection by doing whatever she thought would please him. As she grew older, she excelled in High School academics, earned All-State Honors in choir, and was the best distance runner in her school's history. Even his tiniest affirmation would have filled her emotional need. Yet, with each accolade, medal, or ribbon earned, it was always the same. Dad would give her a vague nod of his head before retreating to his newspaper.

At seventeen, she quit trying. Her grades dropped to C's and choir and track suffered too. Not surprisingly, her faith in God ended. If her own Father didn't love her, why should God?

She shook herself from the past and implored the elevator doors to open. But they remained closed. In a moment of clarity, she realized that this moment was not about her, but about Father. If he was aware of what was happening, she could only imagine his terror and isolation. He needed love, not anger. He needed a calming presence. He needed her now.

She took a shaky breath, shut her eyes, felt the fierce love for him inside her heart. Nothing would ever change that.

She looked around and saw people milling in front of the elevators, talking in hushed tones, waiting to visit loved ones. A young woman walked toward Archer 1 and her name tag said, Tara. The twenty-something female had hair the color of dark chocolate, which was fashionably curled as it cascaded about her slender shoulders.

Tara's inquisitive face, complimented by sky-blue eyes, turned toward Archer 1. On the surface, Tara's expression held an uncommon measure of childlike innocence. Yet, beneath the obvious, lay the aura of an old soul. This unlikely combination whispered softly of purity and purpose.

Tara's eyes sparkled with compassion. "Archer, your elevator's here."

The door opened and Archer 1 swayed slightly, confused by this stranger knowing her name. The young woman placed her hand on Archer 1's forearm and guided her inside. Without asking, Tara pressed the buttons for them. And the door whispered shut.

The elevator lobby number started on five and progressed downward as the elevator rose upward.

I REALIZE IN ARCHER 1'S UNIVERSE that the elevator lobby number starts on five, and then goes backwards as the elevator rises.

How bizarre.

ARCHER 1 LEANED FORWARD, SHOOK HER bewilderment away. "How did you know my name?"

Tara flipped back her long hair, and replied, "Your Father needs you, and there isn't much time."

Tara gave her arm a reassuring squeeze. "I was in line behind you in the lobby and heard you ask for his room number. When someone's in hospice, there's not much time left."

As the elevator rose upward, the bell chimed for the fourth floor, then the third. She glanced into Tara's sky-blue eyes.

Tara lowered her voice, "I died here five years ago and came back as a guide for those who need my help."

Their upward motion ceased, and the elevator stopped on floor two. The door opened and Tara exited into the Neonatal Intensive Care foyer.

Archer 1 hit the elevator door hold button. "You died here? Was it a near death experience?"

Tara glanced over her shoulder, "Miracles happen every day. Never doubt God's mercy."

"I'll believe it when I see it." She removed her finger from the open button and saw Tara wink.

"You might take your ID off unless you want everyone to know your name."

The door finally closed, and Archer 1 shook her head.

Within moments, she arrived on the hospice floor and walked to the workstation. Two female nurses looked up, their faces kind and open.

"Are you here for your father?"

Archer 1 looked down for a long moment. "Yes...." But her voice broke, and she knew her world was about to change forever.

"He's in room fourteen, dear. On the left. If you need us, we're here for you."

As she entered Dad's room, the six-foot, five-inch man she'd known forever was somehow shrunken—had become a shadow of his former self. The faded quality of autumn sunlight extended to the foot of his bed as she crossed over to touch his face. Speckled skin stretched tautly over pronounced bones, yet a quiet dignity remained and spoke softly to her heart. Her soul ached as she encircled his hand with hers. Squeezing lightly, she willed warmth into his cold fingers.

Some arrived in hospice before their journey started, most others at its end. She realized that Dad waited patiently for his moment of profound transition.

Opening her heart one last time, she whispered in his ear, "If only you could tell me, Dad...."

"That he loves you?"

The gentle voice from behind her completed what she could not say.

Archer 1 turned and saw a young wisp of a woman. Her hair, the color of deep mocha, was fashionably curled about slender shoulders. Her inquisitive face, complimented by emerald green eyes, looked up at her. As this young woman moved to Archer 1's side, an expression of uncommon kindness was etched upon her features.

"Tara?" She asked.

The young nurse shook her head no. "You must have met my twin. Her name was Tara, I'm Laura. Tara died here five years ago."

"She told me that when I rode up on the elevator with her minutes ago."

An enigmatic smile graced Laura's lips. But before she spoke, the pervasive hush common to hospice was aborted. Dad gasped and stopped breathing. Archer1's heart dropped, and she touched his face. Seconds later, he drew a shallow breath and relief swept over her.

Laura moved closer. "Focus on your Dad, because there's not much time left."

Archer 1 bent her head and cried, ashamed of her emotional need.

The nurse moved closer, put her arm around Archer 1's shoulders. "I know what you want. It's written on your face and I sense it in your heart. But you have to open a part of yourself that closed long ago."

The grieving daughter looked up into the faded light and saw a lone dust mote floating in midair. Somewhere down the hall a telephone rang five times.

Laura paused. "Just wrap your hands around his and place your fingers in the center of his hands."

Archer 1 took a deep breath and did as Laura instructed. "But how does this work? What do I do?"

"Close your eyes and know God is aware of your need."

The pain of hopefulness caught in her breath. Is it possible? Does God really care?

Archer 1 shifted uneasily. Leaned toward Dad.

Laura took a deep breath. "Imagine an angel holding the same tuning fork in each hand. She strikes one and creates a vibration. That vibration resonates with enough energy to transfer the same pitch and start the second one humming."

Archer 1 pursed her lips. Listened intently.

"When you touch your Dad's palms, you allow divine energy from him to enter your mind. As you rise to his level, a sacred connection forms. Now open your heart to God, and God will open your Father's, too."

A lifetime of pain and disappointment poured into one simple question. Dad, do you love me?

Her thoughts drifted for a moment and then something moved within her. A door opened and an image formed in her mind's eye. An energy, outside her consciousness, resonated with clarity and divine purpose. A subtle light shimmered within, gently illuminating a familiar memory from long ago. She recognized a distant scene from the past. Dad was seated at the breakfast table and thumbed through a scrap book in his lap.

A teenage Archer 1, with teenage attitude, stormed by with teenage indifference on the way out the door.

But this time, the adult Archer 1 sensed a profound change in the memory. This time, the vision revealed what her Father was reading. The first page in his scrap book was a Valentine's Day card she had drawn in the first grade. A worn, yellowed sheet, with bright slashes of red crayon, screamed out, *'I Love U, Daddy.'*

Her father slowly savored each scrap book page and absorbed each newspaper chronicle of her academic and extra-curricular achievements through her school years. He took a sip of coffee, and she felt his pride in her accomplishments.

The awareness of Dad's acceptance was both raw and frightening. But the spiritual connection deepened when she shifted back to the age of six and saw herself in the hospital. Both eyes were bandaged after a complicated eye surgery to correct a serious flaw in her vision. Her world was one of darkness and fear—her only human connection was Dad's quiet presence. But what she couldn't see then as a child, she now saw through this mysterious connection.

For the next twelve days, Dad's face was etched with concern as he sat next to her bed. And when the bandages came off, he walked her out to the car where a dozen balloons were tied to the door handle. She looked up at him, puzzled. Without explanation, he released them into the whimsical breeze. Dad crossed himself, and she could hear his silent prayer. *God, you have guided the hand of her surgeon and given my daughter her sight back. For* each day you watched over her, may these twelve offerings of thanks reach you in Heaven.

He raised his face skyward and watched the balloons drift away. While tears brimmed in his eyes, he had gently guided her into the car.

THE VISION ENDED. ARCHER 1 opened her eyes, removed her hands from Dad's, severing the connection. Awe resonated within her as she looked upon Laura.

The other woman smiled. "I think God has given you a precious gift." The nurse gestured toward father. "And he has, too."

"How did you know what I just saw?"

Laura responded with the same enigmatic smile as before. "Some things are better left unsaid. Just trust in God that he will give you what you need." Laura turned and left the room, leaving her alone with her father.

She walked around to the other side of Dad's bed. Stretched out behind him, curled into his back and pulled him close. Her face burrowed against his neck and she smelled his comforting scent.

His breath was uneven and came in shorter gasps, separated by growing pauses. With each second that passed, her heart drew closer to understanding this quiet man and his silent world within.

Father inhaled. She waited. The air escaped slowly.

Silence plunged in a terrible rush until she heard him breathe again. Then, he patted her hand. "I always loved you, Archer."

She had waited a lifetime to hear those words. With their utterance, a terrible weight lifted from her soul. Her body shook as she held Dad close, and she resonated in a way she never thought possible.

In this moment, if she could see what she felt, it would be a white light amidst a host of angels. She felt the warmth of cascading tears and cried. Cried for the little girl inside. Cried as she made a heartbreaking admission to her Father. "Dad, I thought you didn't care. And when I wished for you to love me, you already did. When I nearly lost you, I found you again."

Tears of joy and sadness ran down her face. She realized that what Tara said on the elevator was true. Miracles happened every day. Archer 1 just believed they couldn't happen to her.

As her Father quietly passed, she would never doubt God's love again.

I AM TOTALLY BLOWN AWAY. INSTEAD of finding Costas, I just experienced a tale of emotional darkness and redemption in the mind of my alternate self. In a parallel dimension. My doppelganger was denied the love she craved, only to realize it was there all the time.

As I look through Archer 1's eyes, Tara comes into the room and Archer 1 stands to face her, next to Dad's bedside. It's the same Tara who has been dead for five years.

"YES, INNER ARCHER, I DIED HERE five years ago, and came back as a servant of the Masters. My job, as the Traveler, is to guide those who visit here and protect the integrity of the alternate dimensions. In spite of the unique separateness of parallel worlds, I am able to project in countless dimensions at will."

The Traveler tapped her finger on the bedside table. "In order to enter an alternate reality, you must focus upon where you want to go, and those around you must be in accord with your desire. When you arrive in a parallel dimension, or any part of earth's current reality, your consciousness can attach to anyone. Or, it can be a free-floating awareness, where you are an intimate observer to other's actions or thoughts."

Tara took a deep breath and smiled. "You are limited to six months in either state. If you stay longer, in a host, you become permanently fixed in their consciousness and the weaker personality will be absorbed by the stronger of the two. You will then live out a natural lifetime and cannot skip from subject to subject to cheat death.

When your awareness travels to an alternate reality, your earthly body remains unconscious and must be tended to if left longer than three hours. If you choose to be a free-floating awareness or attach to another's consciousness, and don't return within six months, your earthly body will die."

Somewhere down the hall, women are talking, then their voices fade to quiet murmurs.

"As you journey into other dimensions, or what some refer to as Elsewhere, you will see that reality is divergent. Sometimes, it is a ragged heartbeat from strange. Other times, a frantic breath from bizarre. Only the intrepid or the curiously insane start their journey here."

Tara narrowed her eyes. "The path to your destiny lies somewhere between sunlight and your darkest fear. A path where darkness leads to hope and concern is the coin of deceit. A path where only love will prevail.

"As you will see, things are different in Elsewhere. Because, in Elsewhere, things are always—off."

I'LL SAY SO. I'M TALKING TO a dead woman. I'm sure pigs can fly in Elsewhere. And, I'm sure, all the ground floor lobbies are labeled the top floor.

TARA IGNORED ARCHER'S MENTAL COMMENTS AND took a deep breath. "Your visit will end shortly. It's important to know that parallel dimensions are like an infinite number of tiny bubbles. Bubbles that are but a heartbeat apart. With each one separate and autonomous of the others. But, if a rift occurs between dimensions, then dramatic changes can affect other worlds."

The woman called Tara stepped back, her face open, yet calmly serious. "Heed my words, Inner Archer. You have a power. A rare gift you're not aware of. Until you understand your hidden ability, you will not find the one called Costas.

But beware of the one who follows you now. One who wishes to enslave you. One who, along with Costas, wants to use your power. Prepare yourself, for this person is approaching now."

I LOOK THROUGH ARCHER 1'S EYES at the wall clock. It

ticks to 12:39, just a minute before my immersion ends. Yet, when I look back, Tara is gone, vanished into thin air.

Muffled footsteps become louder as someone approaches my alternate dad's room. An uninvited visitor moves into the doorway and is dressed in black pants and a starched shirt. His white hair contrasts sharply with his thick, black-framed glasses.

Le Cadavre gives up a wicked grin. "I never got that kiss from you, Archer."

He rushes into the room and triggers his taser.

The device touches Archer 1's torso, and the taut crackle of electricity mutes upon contact. High voltage travels through her body and she twists in agony before tumbling to the floor.

My consciousness, still inside Archer 1's mind, spirals downward on a riot of primal colors.

Before blackness consumes me, I know only one thing.

Le Cadavre has risen from the dead.

20

WHO GOES THERE?

MY LAST CONSCIOUS MEMORY WAS LE Cadavre tasing Archer 1. As I come to, my sight is limited by the flashing red LED lights. Anger pounds through my veins. I scream in rage. Lash out with a vicious right hook. My knuckles collide with flesh, and there's a satisfying crunch.

I shake away the effects of my drug induced immersion, remove the headset and sunglasses, and slowly focus on Slash. He rubs his jaw then grabs my arm. "Why'd you hit me, Arch? Are you crazy?"

Slash is seated beside me in a folding chair next to the couch. I sit up and he lets go of my arm. The look in his eyes startles me when he leans close to my face. "Son of a bitch. What the hell got into you?"

"Ohmygodohmygodohmygod, I'm so sorry. Le Cadavre was tasing Archer 1. And I was slugging him."

"Arch, slow down. This could be a side effect from the pill. But you're safe now. I don't understand what you're saying, so start from the beginning."

I do. For the next thirty minutes he listens closely. When I stop, his eyes are sparkling, kinetic. He leans close, puts his hand upon my cheek. "You did it, Arch, the drug and immersion device works. And the Traveler. Oh, man. A guide and guardian to parallel dimensions. What a freakshow. How about this gift you have? I knew you were amazing, but now you've got some kind of super-power. Something you're not aware of? Sounds like a comic book hero to me."

His enthusiasm is contagious. "It's bizarre, Slash."

"Then there's that cryptic message from the Traveler. Tell me again."

I close my eyes and focus. "I won't find Costas until I claim my destiny and its hidden power. The key to understanding resides in the Traveler's prophecy, where my path lies somewhere between sunlight and my darkest fear. A path where darkness leads to hope and concern is the coin of deceit. A path where only love will prevail."

Slash pushes back his hair. "The prophecy sounds like an English Lit. lecture. You know, the heroine's call to action."

"Have you been smoking weed today?"

"Duh. When do I *not* smoke weed? I do my best thinking when I'm stoned." Slash snaps his fingers. "Look at your thirty minutes in Elsewhere. Archer 1 spent her life in an emotionally dark place. Always trying to please her Father, yet never receiving the love she craved.

"He, on the other hand, adored her, yet was oblivious to her inner needs. Once Archer 1 experienced her Father's hidden feelings, she found that the path through emotional darkness led to hope."

"So what does this mean for me?"

"The message of your immersion is metaphorical. Both Archer 1 and her Father were unaware of each other's emotional state. By extension, you have some weird power, an altered state you're not aware of. I'll bet your next trip to Elsewhere will take you to a place where you never expected to go. A place where concern is the coin of deceit, and only love will prevail."

We both pause, caught up in the insanity of Elsewhere, the Traveler, and an arcane prophecy. Even though it is warm in the apartment, I shiver, and Slash drapes a blanket over me. He reaches under the fabric for my hand, and says, "What about Le Cadavre?"

I squeeze his hand. "We both saw him on the church floor dying from a sucking chest wound. Then his body burned in the fire. There's no way he survived. Unless...."

Slash is a step ahead of me. He removes the two pill bottles from his shirt pocket. "Right here Arch"—he points to the label where the pill quantity is printed—"the thirty-minute bottle says, six." He removes the cap. Looks inside. "We have five left after your trip."

I take the second vial from Slash. Read the quantity out loud. "Two." I shake it and see only one pill inside. My hands tremble. My mind struggles to accept the obvious. My gut says Le Cadavre took the pill before he died because he was waiting for me in Elsewhere. He took the permanent duration drug, and his consciousness is still out there, either as a free-floating awareness or inside a host's mind.

I look out the window, search the street for someone out of place, listen to the pulse of the passing traffic.

The beat of paranoia pounds in my chest. I glance at Slash—*is Le Cadavre hiding inside his mind?*

21

BURN BABY, BURN

SLASH CARESSES MY CHEEK WITH HIS fingers. "Are you ready, Arch?"

It is now six p.m., over five hours since my last trip to Elsewhere. I'm still at Slash's apartment with my head back on his couch pillow. An immersion pill is under my tongue, Dr. Navarro's equipment is in place. But my steely resolve has started to rust.

"Ready to go," I lie. I don't need to burden Slash with my fear. Fear of running into Le Cadavre. Fear of being held hostage to his perverted plans. I cannot trust anyone because his consciousness could be anywhere. Inside Slash's mind, inside the people of Elsewhere. Even within my own mind.

My gut tells me that Le Cadavre is still learning how to move around Elsewhere. But, as time passes, he will get better, and I will too. Until then, I must think smart to direct my consciousness into parallel dimensions. It makes sense to concentrate on the Traveler's prophecy, 'A path where darkness leads to hope and concern is the coin of deceit. A path where only love will prevail.' I can only hope it will take me where I need to go.

The wall clock in Slash's apartment ticks away. His

breathing is steady as he sits next to me and strokes my hair. I appreciate his concern and wait patiently while the pill and Navarro's equipment work together. In a few minutes, my vision goes black, and I hear the distant pulse of a man's voice. A pulse that rises in strength and fervor until it emerges from a background of chaotic chatter.

It is the voice of Brother Hell, the Pentecostal minister from Le Cadavre's transistor radio broadcast.

The preacher comes into focus and I'm standing inside his church, surrounded by an energized congregation. I'm back in Elsewhere and look through Archer 2's eyes. The men and women around her raise their hands and sway back and forth, as if channeling the Holy Spirit.

In a different dimension than Archer and Archer 1, Archer 2, who has a column of bible verses tattooed down both forearms, is mesmerized by, traumatized by, and just plain scared of, Brother Hell.

BROTHER HELL STRODE CONFIDENTLY ACROSS THE raised stage, put his hand to his ear, turned his head from left to right. The ragged lot of lost souls who worshiped him, shifted. Quieted. Leaned forward. He raised his fist upward. "The Bible says to eschew evil, and rock and roll is the devil's music!" The preacher stomped his foot. "This demon music infects our teens with a sickness. A sickness that savages the senses and mauls the moral heartbeat.

"The symptoms of this disease are hideous. Because, it aborts the ethical compass, castrates common sense, and maims decency."

The preacher stared down his congregation, his eyes aflame. Waited for them to flinch. "That ungodly beat, the dark rhythm called rock and roll, is alive. And it will ruin our innocent youth."

The righteous fist-pumped the air. "Amen, Brother!"

Brother Hell took his handkerchief, wiped the sweat from his brow. He leaned forward and shook his finger. "When the beat of the demon got power over your children, they got no will. No will to resist the devil's music. Even somethin' simple as a catchy tune, with a heavy, devil-driven rhythm, can lead to Satan's door."

The crowd's energy grew darker as Brother Hell clenched his fist. "Knock, knock," the preacher said. He cupped his hands around his mouth. "When your children knock, the devil says, come in.

"And when they step inside Lucifer's door, it's like a flock of birds rushin' through. All turnin' at once, instinctively, without contact, appearing led by some invisible source. And that source, that black rhythm, it's the devil's groove. It's come to take your babies in a rush of wind, never to return them home again, never to praise Lord, Jesus. Ever. Again."

The congregation erupted in chaos. Women shrieked. Children cried. Men screamed in rage. Some talked in tongues. Others spun in circles. One lone voice rose above the chaos, "No. More. Rock and roll."

Brother Hell's lost souls took up the chant. *"No. More. Rock and roll. No. More. Rock and roll."*

The crowd surged forward. Filled with hatred, fueled by fear, ready to ignite.

Brother Hell supplied the match.

"Go home." He shook his fist. "Fire is the devil's only friend. Use it to burn your children's records. Records that spread this sickness. And burn them pianos and guitars and drums, too. Destroy the devil's instruments."

The assembly rushed for the doors, hell-bent to drive

the devil out of their children's lives. Hell-bent to recapture some control in their own lives. And hell-bent, just enough, to ignore that they would never change anything. Especially their lives.

Unaffected by the stampeding herd, Brother Hell bowed his head to pray. A slight smile tugged at his lips, because, the good Lord's work was never done.

ARCHER 2 WATCHED THE HYSTERICAL CONGREGATION as they shoved, shouldered, and stumbled their way out of the church. One elderly woman fell, was nearly trampled by the mass of pissed-off humanity, before two men helped her up.

Archer 2 knew the mass exodus brought on by Brother Hell would inflict punishment—punishment upon unsuspecting children for the unbelievable crime of listening to unbelievably good rock and roll.

They pushed her up the aisle and through the door, at the mercy of the mass, until she finally broke free. Archer 2 lurched across the parking lot, stumbled toward the safety of her car, and scrambled inside. Then she locked the doors and took a ragged breath.

Countless times, she had cringed from the passion of Brother Hell as he pounded his Bible, and screamed, "The Bible says...." And when Brother Hell said something, you listened.

Whether you believed it or not.

In the overhead light, she looked at the Bible verses tattooed on her forearms. Wondered where in the good book it said that rock music was evil, or any kind of music for that matter.

Guilt crawled through the oily surface of her fear, squirmed into focus as she white-knuckled the steering wheel. She started the car, put it in gear, turned on the radio. Moved the dial from her favorite rock station to NPR and began to tremble.

The good Brother had always made it clear he was the gate keeper to Heaven, and only the faithful passed through on his watch.

Her breath came in short gasps, once, twice, three times before she could face her terror.

Archer 2 desperately wanted to get into Heaven.

THERE IS A CHANGE IN MY consciousness, and I begin to disengage from Archer 2. I spiral downward in a vortex of color and know my time in Elsewhere is coming to an end. The last thing I hear is Archer 2's cry over a background of depressingly bad classical music.

22

I'LL HAVE ANOTHER HIT, PLEASE

I HAVE BEEN BACK FROM ELSEWHERE for an hour now, and am coming down from a throbbing migraine, possibly a side effect from my immersion. I relate my experience to Slash and he takes a hit off his pipe, holds the smoke in, and lets it out slowly. He has a thoughtful look on his face which changes to surprise.

"I think I understand the Traveler's prophecy."

"Okay, spill it."

"On your first visit to Elsewhere," he taps burnt marijuana from his pipe on to a saucer, "Archer 1 and her Father were unaware of each other's emotional state. And you, by extension, are not aware of an alternate state of consciousness, wherein lies your super-power."

Slash leans over, turns on a table lamp, and asks, "Do you see the parallel?"

"Of course. Are you going somewhere with this?"

Slash steeples his long, slender fingers and stares through me. "Oh, ye of little faith."

The dark shadows cast by the night, linger at the edge of the lamp to my right. Yet, the light of discovery burns bright in Slash's eyes.

"In your second visit to Elsewhere, you encountered

Archer 2, and even more importantly, the charismatic Brother Hell."

I cross my arms.

"Brother Hell manipulated his congregation by inflaming their emotions. He scourged the heart of their fear—the perceived lack of control in their children's lives. The good brother ground the issue of the devil's music in their open wound, all in the name of concern for their youth. His deceit would lead to the destruction of what little relationship remained with their children. All in the name of God."

I uncross my arms and lean forward. Take a moment to think. "The Traveler's prophecy said, I must follow a path where darkness leads to hope and concern is the coin of deceit. A path where only love will prevail."

"Exactly."

"Archer 1's journey through emotional darkness finally lead to hope."

"Go on." Slash pushes his hair back.

"Brother Hell appeared concerned for his congregation but was truly deceitful. He just wanted to spread hatred through his manipulation."

Slash nods and touches my knee. "Arch, this brings you almost full circle. You've experienced two parts of the prophecy. But, there's one more step."

Car headlights illuminate the inside of Slash's apartment, and fade when it passes by. My mind races with the speed of infinity, and I feel the beginning furrows on my brow. "I almost understand, Slash. I'm nearly there."

Slash nods for me to continue.

"My path is to accept an unknown state of mind, and…." My train of thought stumbles. "What about the immersion with Brother Hell, where he showed concern is the coin of deceit? How does that figure with my super-power?"

"What have you learned, Archer? Power can be used for either good or bad. But what is the stronger of the two? History has shown that evil may reign for a season, but ultimately good wins, because it resonates in the hearts of men and women. Tell me, what is another name for the goodness that fills your heart?"

"Love." The answer does not surprise me, because it is the ultimate truth.

Slash smiles. "A path where only love will prevail. Now that you've recognized the meaning in the last part of the prophecy, can you tell me what your path is?"

"To accept my gift and use it to do good."

So simple, yet so profound.

"Exactly, Arch. Now, we're going to find out what your power is, how you can use it, and why Costas and LC are after you."

Slash reaches for his pipe and pulls his sunglasses down. In the meager light, he purses his lips and blows me a kiss. "Not bad thinking for a stoner."

23

RED, RED KROOVY

FOR THE THOUSANDTH TIME, DR. MANUEL Navarro tugged the chain attached to his ankle. There was three feet of play that allowed him limited movement around the cell. Just enough slack to use a small pail to relieve himself or lie upon the sleeping bag on the concrete floor. Far overhead, was a bare, low-wattage bulb that cast a dismal light around his ten by ten lockup. The walls, also of concrete, were stained with what looked like dried blood. The room's only door was steel reinforced, and had a small opening that allowed his food tray in. He had eaten nine times, so he had been here at least three days.

The last thing Navarro remembered, was going out for a pack of cigarettes several days ago and being bludgeoned in a deserted convenience store parking lot around midnight. Before he regained consciousness, he had been stripped down to his underwear, his jewelry and watch taken, and then chained to the floor. He had no idea who his attacker was or what he wanted.

The doctor gripped his chain that was attached to a steel pin anchored in the middle of the floor. He tensed his legs and back then lifted. His muscles strained, his heart thumped like a gangbanger on meth, and the internal rush

of blood burst small capillaries in his face. Navarro kept the
pressure taut, until his hands began to weaken, and tension
eroded his grip.

He dropped the chain and screamed, "What the fuck
do you want with me?"

Sweat rolled down his face, fell onto the floor. Fear and
frustration exploded in his gut as he collapsed. He grabbed
his plastic food tray, threw it at the door, crushed his plastic
cup, and threw it too. His breathing accelerated like a virgins
on her wedding night, his heart power humped the inside of
his chest, then spiked up his throat. All while the cold floor
leached the warmth from his bare legs.

Spittle flew from his mouth. "Show yourself, you bastard!" He slammed his fist into the concrete floor, vicious-
ly, repeatedly, opening small cuts on his knuckles, until a
bloody smear streaked the unforgiving surface. He beat his
other fist, repeatedly against the floor, until all his knuckles
were raw and bleeding.

He cradled his head while blood ran from his lacerated
flesh onto his palms. Navarro dragged his battered hands
down, to his jawline, leaving bloody streaks.

Navarro shrieked with a fierceness that insulted his vo-
cal cords. Air rushed out with no sound attached. Just a
muted explosion of fear, frenzy, and frustration.

His bladder released and Navarro reeled from this final
humiliation. Urine rushed through his underwear, gushed
under his hips, ran down his legs, streamed toward the
drain. He drew his knees up to his chest, wrapped his arms
around his legs, and shivered.

The shivering led to trembling.

He didn't want to die in this place.

The trembling led to shuddering.

He didn't want to die this way.

The shuddering led to bone-shaking spasms.

He didn't want to die in this place, this way, with such indignity.

Dr. Navarro just didn't want to die.

24

IT IS NINE P.M., WELL PAST my dinnertime, but when Slash opens a plastic baggie and drops three zip drives on the couch table, he has my attention.

"These are from Costas' office." He shoves them toward me. "There's one item in particular I want to look at."

Slash mentioned earlier that he'd gotten some 'stuff' from the Director's office, of which the immersion pills and Navarro's device were a part. I pick up the only memory drive with my name on it and get a shiver of anxiety. "Looks like we might have something here." I pass him the memory stick. "Plug it into your laptop. Let's take a look see."

The computer monitor casts a bluish-green glow on his face as he inserts the flash drive. A moment later, a password box dominates the screen.

"Whoa." Slash tugs on his bottom lip. "Any idea what his password might be?"

"You're the psychic puzzle master here, Slash. I'm just window dressing when it comes to this sort of stuff."

"It's gotta be simple, and knowing Costas, it'll be about him."

"So, what does he value most?"

"Besides thinking he's a ladies' man, I'd have to say it's his psychic ability."

I like where Slash's mind is going. "Try typing 'psychic.'"

Slash finger taps it in, presses enter. A red warning box flashes on the screen. "Not good Arch. It says we have one more try. The next one has to be right."

I'm good, really good, with reading people's inner intentions, psychometry, and a shit load of other psychic phenomena, but I never could intuit passwords. "It's got to be something simple, Slash, I just…."

"Sorry to interrupt, Arch. We've got a ticking clock, here. Either come up with a password in the next thirty seconds, or we're screwed."

If I don't get it right, we lose the chance to find something that Costas has hidden. Something with my name on it. Something he doesn't want others to see. I wipe my palms on my jeans and try to think.

"Twenty seconds and counting." Slash's face is pale white in the monitor light.

An intuitive hunch tugs inside me. "It has to be personal and puts Costas in the best light."

"Fifteen seconds."

"Costas in first place."

"Ten seconds."

I snap my fingers, "Psychic one."

"Flesh it out, Arch. Psychic one, or psychic number 1. With or without spaces after psychic. It's gotta be exact or it won't work."

I close my eyes. Clear my mind. A fist appears in my mental imagery with the forefinger sticking up.

"Five seconds. You gotta pull this out, girl."

"Psychic, capital P, no space, and the number 1."

Slash types in *Psychic1*. Hits the enter key. With one second left on the timer, the screen stops flashing.

We both stare at the monitor.

Slash furrows his brow. "Access Granted."

The monitor fills with an image so bizarre, so unexpected, it totally blows us away. We both stare at the screen. "Holy shit!"

25

THIS WON'T HURT A BIT

THE BOLT RELEASED ON HIS CELL'S steel door, and Dr. Navarro raised his head from the concrete floor. The hinges squealed as it swung open and his captor put a large box to the right, just inside the doorway. The man was tall and nude, except for a tan pair of underwear. His entire body was covered with flesh-colored body paint from toe to head. All his hair had been shaved, which gave him the appearance of a living, breathing, mad man.

He stopped a safe distance from Navarro. "Until you are fully trained, you shall call me Father Muerte."

"What the hell am I doing here?" Navarro extended his arms. "What do you want with me?" Father Muerte lunged forward, landing a vicious kick to Navarro's chest. The doctor slammed into the cell wall, his foot chain jerked taut, then curled into a fetal position.

"Remember one thing, Doctor. *I* ask the questions."

"Son of a bitch." Navarro clutched his chest and sat back up.

"I'm going to establish Father Muerte's hierarchy of needs. Being the logical person you are, this should satisfy your need for structure and make your indoctrination go more... smoothly."

"What the hell do you mean?"

Father Muerte slammed his fist in the Doctor's face. "You don't listen well. *I* ask the questions."

Navarro looked up at his bland, flesh-colored captor, shuddered when he connected with the brutal coldness behind the man's eyes. This maniac was capable of anything.

"Now that I have your attention, doctor, let's discuss the levels of need. Based on Maslow's hierarchy, the first need is food, water, and warmth, which will be controlled by me. Second, is your security and safety, which are dependent on your cooperation with my commands. If you disobey, punishment will be swift and severe.

"Next, are the psychological needs—friends and a feeling of accomplishment. Before your indoctrination is over, I will be your only friend. My training will be your greatest accomplishment.

"The final need is the capstone of self-actualization. You will achieve your greatest creative potential. You will become an emotionless, cold-blooded killer, and you will not falter or question my orders. Do so, and I will inflict extreme damage upon your body.

"If you deny my commands, I will incur violence you cannot imagine, pain you cannot escape. If you deny me, your loved ones will die in unimaginably creative ways."

Father Muerte paused, looked at the doctor. "Do not deny me."

Navarro kept his face carefully blank, lowering his eyes. "Understood."

"Then, let the indoctrination begin." He opened his hand to reveal a pill lying in his palm. "Take this."

Navarro knew that his life, as well as his parents and siblings, depended on his cooperation and obedience to this madman's demands. He didn't recognize the generic black capsule. Meaning it could contain any concoction of street or legal drugs. But he knew better than to resist, and his only hope lay in being able to outthink this asshole. He would try to please his captor. Simply put, he would comply—for now.

His hand trembled as he fumbled the pill into his mouth and swallowed it.

Father Muerte watched closely. "Now, we wait."

26

DON'T BLINK

THE SMALL TABLE LAMP IN SLASH'S apartment casts a shallow pool of light, while the rest of the room lies in darkness. The sound of street traffic is nil at this time of night and Slash, and I stare intently at his laptop screen. In the video image, time stamped four weeks ago, Costas and Le Cadavre stand above me, while I lie on a couch in the Director's office.

Costas' voice projects through the computer's speaker, *Archer, you have reached a deep trance state, yet you will go deeper. Relaxing even more as I count down from five to one.*

I glance at Slash. He looks at me. Neither one of us was aware of this hypnotic session, which fuels my sense of violation and unease.

Five, and you feel relaxed as you slide into a pool of liquid warmth. It calms your mind, eases your tension.

Four, as you focus on my voice, your sense of control releases, and your only purpose is to reach the deepest state of relaxation possible.

Three, and all resistance ceases. You surrender to my commands as you go even deeper.

Two, you go deeper still. Your only desire is to follow my instructions.

One, and you have reached a profound trance state. You have only one focus. One desire. To do as I command.

Costas stares intently at my face. *Archer, I want you to reach inside your mind, further than you have before, reach beyond your psychic training, deep into your latent ability. On the count of three, you will go where you have never gone before. You will attain and demonstrate your greatest psychic power.*

One, two, three. You are there.

A vase of flowers flies across Costas' room, smashes on the office floor, to the right of where I'm lying in trance. A happy face, drawn in lipstick is on Le Cadavre's forehead. And the director stumbles to the floor.

Costas stares up at the emoticon on Le Cadavre's forehead. And Le Cadavre stares down at Costas's shoelaces which are tied together.

Le Cadavre rubs at the red lipstick on his forehead. *What the hell just happened?*

The director unties his shoelaces and stands up. He glares at the smashed vase on the floor. *If this is what I think it is, we've stumbled on the greatest exhibition of psychic power ever known.*

This is beyond Nostradamus, Edgar Cayce. Beyond any psychic who ever lived. This is fucking monumental.

Le Cadavre shook his head. *I'm not connecting.*

Look around you. The emoticon, the smashed vase, my shoelaces tied together. I told Archer to do something spectacular. And she did this.

But how?

Costas nodded in understanding. *I gave her a command, and she somehow stopped time, smashed the flower vase, applied lipstick to your face, tied my shoelaces together, all within seconds. She did what no living person has ever done. She stopped time. She stopped time and we didn't see a damn thing.* He waved his hand across the room. *We've got to keep a lid on this. Can you imagine the potential here? Once we get Archer to show us how this is done, then all the world's wealth is ours.*

Le Cadavre stroked his chin thoughtfully. *Will she remember what happened?*

I'll give her a post hypnotic command to block her memory of this session. While I do that, I want you to stop the closed-circuit camera. Remove the memory stick. Replace the original with a blank just to be safe.

The video goes black on the laptop screen, and Slash leans back. "Holy shit. No way, Arch. You can stop time?"

If this is true, Costas and Le Cadavre just opened Pandora's Box, and only bad things can come from it. They will try and torture the secret from me. A secret that I have no conscious memory or knowledge of.

And when that fails, they will kill me.

But I will not wait for them. I will not fear them. Because I will take the fight to them, on my terms and conditions. Then, I will crush them.

27

STINKIN' SNAKES

DR. NAVARRO HAD EXPERIMENTED WITH DRUGS in the 60's and the 70's. Marijuana, acid, and a bagful of others, but what Father Muerte had given him an hour ago was the mother of all substances. His senses and mental acuity were eerily enhanced. The doctor could smell, no, taste his captor's personal scent mixed with the painted-on body color. A combination of tart acidity married to industrial chemicals. He noticed the telltale pulse of blood in Father Muerte's temple, the harsh calmness of his breathing. There was a layer of colors that wavered over his captor's body, something he had read about, but never experienced. An aura, what the New-Agers called the visual energy imprint.

The doctor was fucked up and knew it. More so than a couple lines of coke. More than an acid trip. More messed up than he had ever been, doing any kind, or combination of drugs. The fact was, he was so fucked up that it scared him.

Father Muerte checked his watch. "It has been an hour and I believe you're fully immersed in the drug's effect."

Navarro shifted on top of his sleeping bag. He nodded his head obediently because it was expected. The smell of his urine in the small cell was overpowering, but the scent of his fear was strangely comforting. Comforting because it wouldn't let him forget his situation, wouldn't let him relax his vigilance.

"Doctor, you're experiencing a designer drug created by my mentor's employer, the federal government. It is a precise cocktail of oxytocin, plus the stress inducing effect of methamphetamine, and the distilled essence of a substance found only in the Amazon rain forest."

Navarro nodded his head again.

"You will not remember our conversation, which is why I'm being informative. The specific combination of drugs will aid in your conversion and be active in your system for the next three days. The effect you're experiencing now is pleasurable. I've taken the drug myself, so I speak from experience. Yet, in a few minutes, the pleasure will be replaced with total, abject fear. Fear like you have never experienced. Fear intensified by a magnitude of terror that has killed the weak-willed. So, for your sake, doctor, pray for strength.

"In this drug cocktail, the methamphetamine enhances your stress, while the oxytocin creates an emotional bonding. The third ingredient blurs the part of the brain that distinguishes between right and wrong. Your inhibitions will be defenseless as you bond and embrace the horror I'm about to release. From this one pill, you'll experience unimaginable terror and ecstasy sporadically for the next three days. Thanks to your Facebook page, I know what you fear most."

Father Muerte picked up the large, cardboard box he had brought in earlier. Placed it in front of Navarro.

The frenzied motion within the container conjured the worst possible nightmare in the doctor's mind. He slid away from the box until his ankle chain stopped him. Navarro knew what was inside.

"You've heard of the movie *Snakes on a Plane?*" Father Muerte snickered. "Well, get ready to say hello to these angry fellows."

He dumped the contents on the floor. "If it's any consolation, they're non-poisonous."

Snakes exploded out of the container. Little snakes, long snakes, large snakes. They were writhing, squirming, twisting, turning and heading toward him.

"But, wait, doctor. Let's amp your fear." Father Muerte pulled a small remote from his pocket, pressed a button, plunged the room in darkness.

Navarro felt the first snake slither up his bare leg.

He screamed, and more cold-blooded reptiles surged toward him. Drawn to him, pulled to his warmth, attracted to his fear. They swarmed over his exposed flesh, slithered up his chest, into his face. Paralyzed by the cold, writhing mass of slimy flesh, he finally beat at the heap of squirming snakes on his torso. Flinging them into the wall, tearing them from his face.

He threw another snake away, and five more took its place. Navarro was engulfed, smothered, overpowered, by the unending onslaught. He shrieked as snakes nipped his face, his arms, his chest. Blind, and chained to the floor, he finally collapsed. There was no place to move, nowhere to hide.

His heart pulsed. It pounded. It rumbled and roared. A furious rhythm raged deep inside his chest. He sucked in harsh, jagged, gasps of air. Shards of internal light flashed behind his closed eyes.

The slimy reptiles still swarmed over his body, rubbed their oily flesh against his, squirmed through his underwear, and covered his face and mouth. Then the unthinkable occurred.

The horror, the terror, the fear.

Stopped.

Then it was replaced with an emotion Navarro was unprepared for. One that he couldn't understand, or fathom.

As much as he had resisted the snakes before, he now was drawn to them, hugging the pile on his chest. He scissored his legs, creating friction between his flesh and the writhing bodies.

Father Muerte turned the light back on.

Navarro embraced the squirming heap, flushed with unimaginable joy. Rolling from side to side, he was ecstatic in newfound love.

Father Muerte looked down. "Welcome to the world of fear and love, doctor—where you will never be the same again."

28

DO YOU TRUST ME?

I CURL UP NEXT TO SLASH on his couch, and sigh. "I couldn't have survived the past few weeks without you."

He puts his arm around my shoulders and draws me close. The patter of rain upon the roof is calming, and the wind buffets against the windows. Slash's heartbeat bumps against his chest, comforting me with its steady rhythm. He leans in and kisses the top of my head.

"You've been through a lot, Arch and I couldn't be prouder of you."

His blond hair hangs down in his eyes, and I brush it back. "Thanks for keeping me safe."

"We'll move tomorrow, a small garage apartment across town. Thanks to a friend who owes me a favor. With Costas still out there—and the possibility of Le Cadavre's consciousness being around—we can't be too careful."

I snuggle closer to him.

"Tomorrow is a new day, and you can do another immersion to track down that bastard, Costas."

Slash's eyes sparkle in the low light, and I reach for him again, draw his lips toward mine. Kiss him softly and rest my head against his chest.

His breath comes in gentle waves as he caresses my hair

with his hand. My Alpha bad boy has a uniquely gentle side that he works hard to conceal. Slash hides his sensitivity by playing the stoner role, one that tricks people into judging him as a loser. He's anything but that.

Slash graduated from high school at thirteen and college when he was sixteen. He is also a psychic savant and one of the top telepathists in the country. His parents, who were in the psychic espionage program with mine, were selected because of their unique abilities, as well as their son's. Both Slash and I were being groomed as the next gen participants in the government's clandestine psychic warfare project. But now, with Costas gone, it is anyone's guess whether the project will continue.

"It's late, Arch." Slash stretches. "The bed's all yours. I'll take the couch."

"You can sleep with me."

"Don't think I could keep my hands off you, princess. I don't have to be psychic to see that your tired tonight."

Slash spreads a blanket over his body and lays his head on a pillow. I step out of his sight, pick up the immersion pill bottle from the end table, and slip it inside my jean's pocket. One hour ago, I had secretly transferred Navarro's device to the bedroom and my sexual offer to Slash was a ruse. I knew he would refuse.

I walk around him to the bedroom. "Love ya, honey."

"Love ya, too."

I close the door, lean against the wall, shut my eyes. Try to slow my racing heart. By taking the pills and equipment, this marks the first deception I've engaged in with Slash, and it hurts to the marrow. Our relationship has been founded on trust, but I have a good reason to do an immersion on my own. If things work out, I will confess tomorrow.

If things don't work out, that means something nasty hit the fan and I won't be around to explain what happened.

29

TIME ON MY HANDS

MY HEART IS POUNDING AS I lean against the bedroom wall. A night light casts a small halo of incandescence by the head of his bed, just enough for me to walk over there. My deception with Slash has me bummed out, but my gut tells me I'm doing the right thing.

I turn back the comforter, take off my shoes and settle under the covers. The bottle of pills is in my hand and I pray that my intuition is correct.

In my first Elsewhere immersion, the Traveler said that I must direct my thinking and focus upon a desired location. If someone else is present during my transition phase, their thoughts must be in accord with mine.

In the world of psychic phenomena, thoughts have power, they have force, they have substance. Thoughts are things, and in their own reality, can influence an outcome. When accessing an Elsewhere location, if all thoughts are not in accord with the journeyer, then by their lack of unity, they will change the seeker's direction.

It's imperative to focus on where I want to go. I'm choosing to do this alone, because Slash's thoughts could affect my outcome.

I get out of bed and quietly move to the door where I

crack it open an inch. Slash is fast asleep and doesn't suspect a thing. I'm doing this trip while he sleeps in order to avoid his objections to my going it alone.

I will pursue my direction.

I will see the Traveler.

I will learn how to stop time.

And, I will do it now.

I return to the bed, put the pill under my tongue and turn Navarro's equipment on.

30

A PLACE ABOVE TIME

I AM NO LONGER AT SLASH'S, but I am aware and suspended in total darkness. There is no foundation beneath my feet, no touch of wind upon my face. Yet, I experience a feeling of breathtaking motion, of incredible movement through this void. I sense a timeless presence that permeates this dark theatre yet sheds no light upon its stage.

Time, time, time, I mentally repeat. My focus is strong and true. Unwavering and committed. Still, I fly through Stygian darkness. Toward the understanding of a gift I never asked for. Toward a person called the Traveler. Toward destiny.

The darkness around me, which is part of a greater power, expands. Inhales. Then breathes out. On the feathered edge of this exhalation, starlit, phosphorescent trails rush past me with fantastic speed. Trails that leave upon me a fingerprint of latent energy. Felt like the touch of a pleasant memory, passing through my clothing, my body, and face.

In the heart of this dense theatre, where movement is instantaneous, yet impossible to measure, where the luminous trace of a knowing presence passes through my body, I repeat, 'Time, time, time."

The words echo in my mind.

I'm within the beginning and end of that which cannot be touched. I am part darkness. Part fabric of time, and I am luminosity, the thread that binds it together.

I am one and all. For, I am in the birthplace of time.

I AM AWARE, BUT NO LONGER suspended in total darkness. A firm foundation rests under my feet and the soft, sweet breath of wind moves my hair. The faint outline of a door appears in front of me, suggesting a source of light on the other side. I reach for the doorknob, twist it, and pull it toward me.

A wall of sparkling moonbeams pours in a sheet from the top of the door, down to the floor, where it disappears. I pause until a female hand extends through the shimmering white veil from the other side, and beacons me inward.

I inhale deeply, close my eyes, and take a few steps. When I reopen them, I'm surprised to see the door I just walked through is now closed. The cascading barrier of moonlight is gone and with a quick look through a nearby window, I'm inside a second story bachelor's apartment. That is, if the smell of pot and a selection of *Playboy* magazines is any indication of gender.

"Nice to see you again, Archer." Tara, the Traveler has an inquisitive look in her sky-blue eyes.

"Good to see you, too."

Tara flips back her long brown hair back. "Bet you have some questions, don't you?"

"Hell, yes. Where have I been and where am I now?"

Tara spreads her hands. "When you took the immersion pill and engaged the induction device, your conscious direction put you at the source of time."

"How did you know I started the journey?"

"The Dimensional Architect allows me oversight over all that happens within alternate dimensions as well as the realm of time."

"And now," Tara gives an expansive sweep of her arm. "I welcome you to a place above Time."

I look at the living room's dinghy walls, the outdated shag carpet, the crusty bong and cigarette butts in overflowing ashtrays. "How can I be above time?"

"You're in an apartment above Time Chemical, a company who rents out these digs by the semester, mostly to college students with a tight budget and a taste for cheap marijuana."

Tara evidently sees the confusion on my face, exactly what I feel inside. "It's a visual metaphor, Archer. Since the human eye cannot see 'time,' the Dimensional Architect created Time Chemical and the apartment above, to help visitors get a view on an abstract concept."

I mull that over. "So, when I left the grand cavern of time, and stepped through the door, I entered this apartment?"

"Yes."

"An apartment above Time Chemical? I'm literally *and* figuratively in a place above Time."

"True. And when you enter any of its infinite rooms down the corridor, you can stop time if you choose to."

"Is this where I came when Costas hypnotized me a month ago?"

"The exact same place."

"How did I get back to his office and heave the flower vase? And do the other stuff, too?"

Tara points toward a closed door on the opposite side of the living room. "The renter of this apartment, when he's not in classes, is your guide to time. He takes you wherever you want to go. His name is Ed Martin, but, prefers, 'Mister Ed.'

"All travelers enter the heart of time first, then go through the door to enter a place above Time. Mister Ed takes them to their stated destination. In your case, he led you to the correct door, and you entered Costas' office. In which time was suspended and you could do whatever you wished."

"Wow, that's a lot to take in," I gesture toward the living room. "When I do an immersion, I'm either a free-floating consciousness or attached to a host. So, how do I have a body now?"

Tara steps close, places her hand on my arm. "This is your astral body, a manifested form somewhere between your soul and physical body. But remember, if your astral body dies, then your earth body dies, too."

I touch my lips, "Seems real enough to me. But I have another question. Is my ability to travel here and stop time anywhere I choose, my super-power?"

"One and the same."

"How did I get here the first time when Costas hypnotized me?"

"He gave you a hypnotic suggestion and you naturally accessed your latent ability. Then your astral body manifested itself and you did your mischief."

"Do I need an another immersion trip to stop time when I'm not hypnotized?"

"You don't need it anymore. All you must do is visualize the doorway at the heart of time, and that will lead you to the place above Time. From there you can access the dimensions, as well as anywhere on Earth, by either attaching to another entity or becoming a floating awareness. You can still stop time, too. Even though the immersion pill you took tonight helped you to focus on your destination, you're still tied to its thirty-minute limit."

My head spins, and I have a thousand questions. "I've found what my power is, So, what is my destiny? What does it mean to me?"

Tara looks straight ahead. "You have traveled to a place where time can be stopped, and unfortunately, your time is almost up."

A kaleidoscope of color swirls before my eyes, and the Traveler nods. "Your destiny is to use your ability for the good of all, Archer."

The darkness opens before me and I begin the journey back to my place and time, with some real concerns.

31

HAIRY LITTLE CREEPERS

DR. NAVARRO JERKED AWAKE, AND REALIZED he was in a hospital bed. With a crisp, linen sheet tucked up under his chin, he took a very deep breath. The small room had a cloth privacy screen between his bed and the next one. Deep breathing came from the other side, and Navarro assumed his roommate was asleep. However, he offered a tentative, "Hello?"

A muted television, mounted by the ceiling in front of him, was on a financial news network, and posted current stock prices. The hospital suite's outside door was closed and Navarro listened for foot traffic, or sign of a nurse. Momentarily, a linen cart squeaked and bumped its way past his frosted glass door, then continued down the hallway.

The doctor glanced at his bedside table where a Styrofoam water container rested next to his cup. A straw lay against the cup's inner side, the tip of which had lipstick imprints where someone had taken a sip of water.

For the first time, he wondered why he was here. Had there been an accident? Some catastrophic illness? He couldn't remember the past several days because everything was a blank. The nurse's call button was on the bedside table next to the TV remote. When he tried to pick it up, he couldn't move his right hand. The doctor jerked again and heard the clank of metal. Within moments, he realized that all four limbs were cuffed to the reinforced bed rails. Stranger still, his legs were spread eagled and a slight bulge rose under the sheet just above his kneecaps.

"Nurse. Hello? I need help."

Another linen buggy rolled by, creating a visual smudge through the room's frosted glass door.

"Help. Someone, please help me!"

The sleeping patient next to the doctor snorted, and Navarro heard the crunch of a mattress as someone rolled off the bed.

The privacy screen pulled back and Navarro squeezed his eyes shut, then reopened them. His roommate was a man dressed in a female nurse's outfit, complete with white, rubber soled shoes, beige stockings, and a pointed brassiere under the uniform that would make Madonna jealous. His face and head were completely hairless and covered with a thick layer of flesh-colored body paint. Brilliant, red lipstick had been applied to his generous lips, a trace reddening one front tooth.

"You're awake, doctor. You're probably wondering who I am. So, just call me Father Muerte."

"What the fuck is going on? Who are you and why am I cuffed to the bed?"

"You're in the final day of your 'indoctrination,' doctor. And watch your mouth. You're in the presence of a lady."

"Just what is going on? Why am I handcuffed?"

"Thanks to a designer drug I gave you yesterday, you're being molded into my single-minded student, one who will do my bidding." Father Muerte held a yard stick in his right hand and lifted the bed sheet off Navarro. Nestled between the doctor's knees was a small plastic kitchen bag. Which seemed to have a life of its own, and that worried

Navarro. Something was inside. Whatever it was, was obviously pissed off and wanted out. By the position of the plastic bag, the opening would disgorge its contents directly onto his crotch.

To make matters worse, his nurse, the Rocky Horror Picture Show, cross dressing alien, began prodding the sack, causing the contents to move in a manner that promised endless horror. Navarro gritted his teeth as sweat rolled down his brow.

Father Muerte said, "You have witnessed and endured one of your two mortal fears—the snakes were first, doctor. Soon, I will introduce you to the last one."

Navarro couldn't remember a thing, but he let out a howl and jerked his cuffed limbs.

"It won't do any good to try and get free, doctor. Steel continues to be stronger than flesh and bone."

Father Muerte jabbed the garbage bag with his yard stick again, and the sack opened slightly.

The doctor raised his head to look at the plastic bag between his legs. He no longer had his underwear on and was completely naked. Totally vulnerable to whatever was trying to get out of the sack.

"The second of your worst fears, doctor are the creepy crawly, eight-legged kind. Hairy, fuzzy, bristly, and bald. These spiders should remind you of a special memory. I read an interesting tidbit on your child protective services report. The authorities said when you were four years old, your father locked you in a closet. A dirty, nasty, bug-infested enclosure, where you were repeatedly bitten by a nest of poisonous spiders. Nearly died from it, didn't you?"

Navarro strained his neck to see what was coming out of the sack.

"You see, I have thousands of spiders in this sack between your legs. They have enough poison to toast your genitals. Then, the hairy little fellows will work their way up to your chest, your face, and your head."

Navarro couldn't cry out. But he silently bit his lower lip to keep from expressing fear. The childhood memory of being locked in the closet rushed to his mind—the spider's web that stuck to his face when his father shoved him inside. The multiple spider bites on his hands and arms. The emotional torment was devastating and the physical pain from the bites, excruciating, until the unbearable abdominal cramping started.

For Navarro, that memory had enough horror to last the rest of his life, but his terror quotient multiplied when Father Muerte stuck his yardstick into the bag again. The sack opened enough to let a trickle of spiders out. They immediately started climbing Navarro's inner thighs.

The doctor felt a prickling sensation down below, and he jerked his head up to see a mass of spindly legs, swollen abdomens, and unblinking eyes crawling up his pubic hair.

Father Muerte opened the plastic sack fully and shook its contents into the space between the doctor's legs.

Navarro tried to move, but the cuffs around his ankles were securely fastened to the bed rail. Then, the spiders started to crawl over him. Biting in the most sensitive places, they delivered a sharp, piercing infliction that crippled him with pain. He gasped for air, and his whole body shook.

Five ounces of writhing, squirming, spiders covered his penis and testicles. Under their quivering mass, the arachnids continued to savage him with a vengeance. The frantic energy shifted, and the mound moved with a life of its own.

The doctor screamed. His neck tendons stretched taut, his lips peeled back and exposed gum and teeth. The spiders feasted upon him, scuttling, scurrying, and savoring the sweet flesh before them. Their scissor-like jaws cut at the sensitive skin—skin that was totally exposed to the thriving mass of spiders.

Father Muerte opened the hospital's frosted glass door, and the total insanity of his situation rammed home. The doctor saw a large movie projection screen outside his room. Momentarily, an image of a wheeled linen cart traveled the length of the screen, along with the squeaky-wheel sound effect.

"You see, doctor, there is no one here to help you. No nurse, no other patient, no one who really cares. Just an old transvestite with a penchant for inflicting drama and pain."

Navarro's heart thudded, thumped, thundered, and pounded itself into a critical overload of fear-induced beats. His breath hiccupped in a bastard syncopation with his heartbeat. He was just one step from cardiac arrest.

He bucked his body and the pulsing mass of spiders squirmed over his lower stomach.

He arched his back and the spiders began to spread up his chest.

He shook his head from side to side, watched the eight-legged monsters creep up to his neck.

Navarro blew them away with a burst of air. However, more took their place. Still, no relief came.

His body shuddered and the doctor knew he was going to die.

With that thought, the pain eased, dissolved its' hard-outer edge, dissipated under the weight of something bigger than his torment.

The agony and fear eroded and was replaced with a blissful eruption—a sense of connection with something larger than himself. In that moment of transition, Navarro knew. Knew in his heart, knew in his bones, that he was soul bound to Father Muerte in a way more powerful than mere emotion.

Navarro realized his torment was a pathway to a great emotional epiphany. A personal connection ignited by pain, and intimate suffering, which birthed a bond of love for his teacher, and tormentor.

Father Muerte was attuned to his pupil's transition and knew the final, inner wall had been breached. He gently swept the spiders from Navarro's body and covered his student with the linen sheet. "Doctor, I lied about the spiders. They aren't poisonous, and the bites you received, while sensitive, will heal."

Tears flowed down Navarro's cheeks. "Damn the injury. The pain was my catalyst to form this connection. The love I have for you is beyond words. I forgive you for your actions. For you have brought me to enlightenment, a place I've never imagined. A place where my soul is reborn, my love unbridled. For that, I would give my life for you."

Father Muerte wiped the doctor's tears away. "Before things are over, you'll do exactly that."

32

A DOUBLE TAP TO THE HEAD

AS I COME TO FROM MY immersion, I open my eyes and begin thrashing my arms and legs. Slash is sitting next to the bed and lays his body on top of mine to limit my motion. Within a few minutes, I stop and regain my equilibrium. He raises and disappointment etches his face. Even though he is one of the top mind readers in the country, it shouldn't surprise me that he saw past my deception and got inside my thoughts. I don't know whether to be guilty over getting caught, or relieved that he cares.

"You've got some explaining to do, Arch." He removes my headset and sunglasses and picks up the bottle of immersion pills. His nostrils flare and a blood vein pulses in his temple as he leans closer. "You could have been hurt, or something might have gone wrong." He shakes the pill bottle. "If you don't care about yourself, don't you care a little about me? I've been going crazy with worry. To just sneak off and do a thirty-minute trip without backup is foolish. If I weren't here to tend to your convulsions, you could have hurt yourself. Why'd you do the immersion?"

I meet his gaze and think about being tortured by Le Cadavre. Think about how Slash saved my life. How he was a big part in fixing me in the weeks after it ended. I keep my voice flat, "When I first met the Traveler, she said that I must focus on where I want to go in an alternate dimension, or current reality. The people around me need to have the same focus. Slash, I just wanted a pure trip to discover my super-power. I didn't want any extraneous thoughts, your thoughts, to sabotage my immersion. That's why I didn't tell you." I place both hands on his shoulders. "Can you forgive me?"

It has always been hard to get a read on Slash, he hides his thoughts so well, yet the look of disbelief on his face tells me that my actions hurt him very badly.

His eyes tighten around the corners. "I guess this is where it's easier to beg for forgiveness, than to ask for permission?"

"If you go to Webster's dictionary, look under b, and go down to busted, you'll see my name. I admit it, you got me, Slash. I'm guilty as charged."

The corners of his eyes relax, and laugh lines appear as he smiles. He takes a quick glance at his watch. "Since you're up, what say you take a trip and find Costas?"

Slash has gone one-eighty on me. From pissed off to totally mellow. It is times like this that I realize how little I know him. That's not a bad thing, though. In fact, it's sexy. I can't think of a better person to be with as I pull him toward me.

AFTER OUR LOVEMAKING, I HAD FILLED Slash in on the place above Time and my super-power, much to his amazement. I step out of his shower, into a fresh set of clothes, and finish drying my hair with a towel. When I enter the bedroom, he is sitting on a chair next to the bed, pats the mattress, and beckons me over.

"Arch, it's 3:00 a.m. and now is the best time to find Costas. He's likely to be fast asleep. So, just remember that you have two options when you find him. I suggest that you focus on becoming a free-floating awareness instead of landing in his mind. He'll be on the offensive if he discovers your presence. We don't know what action he can take if he detects you. Never underestimate him. Be careful."

I squeeze his hand. "Thanks. And I love you."

"Love you, too."

Since I don't need an immersion pill, or Navarro's induction device, I mentally repeat the words, Costas, Costas, Costas. Free-floating awareness.

Slash's head is turned toward me, his eyes are closed, and he appears to be deep in thought. Good, he is focused on my trip.

Minutes pass and I struggle with my emotions. Costas is an unknown factor, and what could Slash do if something happened to me? How would he even know? There are so many variables that could go wrong, and that leaves a trace of unease in my mind.

I am back on track with my focus, and soon, I enter the Hallway of Time, concentrating on my destination. Momentarily, the effects of the immersion leave me as a free-floating awareness inside a beach-front house. I don't have a body, but I'm consciously aware, and in command of my senses. To my left, an open bedroom window allows the moonlight inside. The rich aroma of ocean spray fills the room, and I hear the gentle lapping of waves upon the nearby shore. A digital clock on the bed's nightstand reads 3:10 a.m.

The height that I am observing the room—or, my center of being—is around my normal stature of five foot, ten inches.

I wonder about mobility. So, I think left, and like a

camera panning that way, the floor shifts as if I were walking across it.

A soft snore comes from the figure sleeping on the bed and I advance toward him. As I hover over his head, it's the bloatus blossom himself. Allen Costas, former Director of Psychic Espionage, now fugitive on the run.

If I could spit on this bastard, I would. My awareness is inches above his face, and I smell garlic in his exhalations, as well as the fish he had for dinner tonight. I look at the scum who ordered my parent's deaths, a man who almost sold out his country's secrets, a man who almost got away with it all. If I were here, in body, it would be so easy to put a bullet in his head. Dump the corpse fifteen miles offshore. No one would be the wiser.

Something spikes within my consciousness, and an option presents itself. I project my awareness inside the sleeping Costas' chest and form a connection. The unsuspecting murderer doesn't stir as I psychically sense his heart, beating slowly and rhythmically.

I use my mental connection to squeeze the muscular organ, and the pressure causes Costas to stir, but not waken. He coughs and turns in his sleep.

When my psychic grip on his heart tightens, the heartbeat increases. Costas takes a deep breath and I project a mental sedative on his consciousness. He kicks the covers back, exposes his bare flesh to the restless breeze through the window.

His heart pumps rapidly, and I amp the pressure. The man who killed my parents will be dead in a minute. There will be no witnesses to the crime. The autopsy will erroneously conclude a heart attack.

No one will know how he really died.

I apply more pressure.

No one will know why he died.

I tighten my psychic stranglehold.

No one will ever know the truth.

No one, except me.

His cardiac rhythm rages rapidly and a dark pleasure ripples through my awareness. I compress my enemy's heart in a mental death-grip. Feel it thrash in his chest, hear his lungs gasp for air, watch his legs kick frantically.

I bring Costas to the edge of death.

A moment before he goes into cardiac arrest, I release my mental hold. The heartbeat is still dangerously high, his body covered in sweat. For the next fifteen minutes I observe his declining heart rate, until it returns to normal.

I was so close to killing him, and it could have been the perfect crime. No one would ever know the truth. With another ten seconds of pressure, he would have died. His death, however pleasing though, won't bring my parents back. My action shows more humanity than he offered Mom and Dad when he ordered their deaths.

It will be up to the courts to weigh Costas's actions and decide his fate. Not me.

I move my awareness out of the bedroom and into the small dining room. On the breakfast table, I find what I'm looking for—some junk mail, labeled occupant. I lower my center of being until I can read the address. That is enough to seal Costas's fate.

My mission is complete, and I start to will myself back to my body. Just before I exit the beach house, I notice an object on the breakfast table. An object that puts a terrifying spin on the situation with Costas. An object that will benefit him immensely.

33

GUESS WHO?

THE INSTANT I WAKE FROM MY immersion, I shoot up from the bed, grab Slash's arm. "I know where Costas is, get the police on the phone, now!"

"Give me a second, Arch." Slash gets the number, calls the Amarillo PD and is transferred to a night-shift supervisor. He informs the officer about Costas and the ongoing homicide investigation.

I grab some paper, scribble the Florida address down, and push it into his hands. Slash relays the information to the supervisor. Through the phone's ear speaker, I hear the officer ask, "How did you find his current location?"

"An undisclosed source." Slash looks at me and we both know the truth would be impossible to believe. The explanation seems to satisfy the officer, who takes Slash's name, address, and phone number before ending the call.

My boyfriend sits back in his chair. "The supervisor said that he'll contact the police department in Marco Island, Florida and have them arrest Costas immediately."

"It can't be soon enough because what I saw at his place could change the whole situation."

Slash's eyebrows raise and he leans toward me. "What is it, Arch? What did you see?"

"I saw…." Before I finish, an object crashes through the bedroom window and rolls to the edge of the nightstand. It's a nasty-looking, aerosol-sized device and I don't have to be psychic to know it's going to explode. Slash and I dive across the bed for protection just as the apparatus detonates. A blinding flash of light is followed by a deafening, concussive explosion.

The flash-bang grenade sends me tumbling off the bed and onto the floor. I'm totally blind. Totally deaf. Totally disoriented. Within seconds, an intruder's strong hands jerk me up, fasten a hood over my head, and put on wrist cuffs. Then I feel the discharge of a large-caliber gun near my torso.

I scream, "Slash!" And hear nothing. My auditory system is still in shock. His safety is all I can think about and I pray to God he hasn't been shot. Or killed. I can't bear to think of the man I love lying dead.

My aggressor throws me over his shoulder, carries me outside to an idling vehicle, and dumps me in the trunk. My thoughts are racing, and I'm terrified beyond words. Until I overcome the total disorientation of the flash bang, I'm unable to fight back. The rough cloth over my head fuels my claustrophobia, incites rapid breathing, and leaves me light-headed. My heart pummels the inside of my chest and my breath bursts in and out. Beads of sweat roll down my brow and upper lip. I'm engulfed in total darkness—alone, afraid, aching.

The car slams into gear, burns rubber, and throws me across the trunk. Several quick turns later, the driver accelerates onto the open road.

During the next few minutes of high-speed travel, I frantically search for a tire tool, a car jack, anything to use as a weapon. The vehicle I'm in is an older model without an inside trunk release, or a back seat that I can kick out.

The vehicle slows and begins to rumble across an unpaved road. Momentarily, we come to a stop. The driver's door opens, and my impaired hearing barely discerns the crunch of footsteps on gravel approaching the trunk. I feel the car shift as another person leaves the vehicle and walks away.

It's good to know what I am facing. There are two abductors, which complicates any kind of escape.

The trunk pops open and the cool, night wind brushes against my arms and neck. It is several hours before dawn and the world is still dark, particularly so with a sack over my head. My captor pulls me out of the trunk, slings me over his shoulder. Judging by my limited senses, he is tall and muscular. At this point, I'm still too disoriented to fight, so I must wait until my senses fully return.

It is a short distance down the gravel path before we go up a few steps and through a door. After we enter, the flat scuff of his shoes on concrete marks our trail. I deduce that we're probably in a secluded metal building, on the outskirts of Amarillo, perhaps in a deserted industrial setting.

My captor drops me in a gritty, wooden chair, removes my cuffs, duct tapes my feet and hands to its legs and arm rests. He pulls off my hood and I suck in a quick breath, detect the odor of stagnant water and the scent of my own fear. It has been about thirty minutes since I got hit by the flash bang, and I now have partial use of my sight and hearing. Of that I'm relieved.

My abductor moves close. "You have something my teacher needs, and I will be the one who gets it for him."

The voice is familiar, and I struggle to place this man. I know him. "Who is your teacher? What does he want from me?" My voice is raspy, coated with a rusty edge of fear.

The teacher steps out of the shadows and into the dim light of a single bulb. "I am the one Le Cadavre named Father Muerte."

My sight is clearer now, and I see a tall, nearly nude man with flesh-colored paint over his hairless body. My gut squirms because this whole scene is a real freak show. Who dresses like a freakin' weirdo? That little voice in my head answers, "Someone who has nothing to lose, someone insane." Getting out of here alive, doesn't look promising at all.

He crosses his arms. "Before my acolyte is through with you, you will divulge your secret. You will show me how to stop time."

I stare at the body-painted creep. Then his partner. In the tinsel glow of the single bulb, I finally recognize Father Muerte's assistant.

My leg muscles tighten. I have no way to run.

My mouth goes dry. I have no water to quench it.

My mind moves too rapidly. I have no way to slow it.

My soul begs me to scream. I have no voice.

Finally, I whisper, "Doctor Navarro?"

He bows at the waist. "So good to see you, Archer."

34

TWO CRUISERS FROM THE MARCO ISLAND PD pulled up to Costas's address with lights off and cut their engines before they reached the driveway. Four officers in body gear got out, checked their equipment and drew their weapons. The entry specialist mounted the porch steps, positioned himself with a partner, and heaved a seventy-pound entrance-buster into the hollow core door, splitting it down the middle.

Eight-hundred pounds of testosterone enhanced, and armed alpha males stormed the home, screaming in unison, "Police!" Marco Island police!" They quickly searched the living area, flashlight beams bouncing around the room, but found no suspect.

The kitchen and living area were immediately cleared. The only bedroom, when entered, showed a slept in bed, but no Costas. The officers checked the closets as well as the bathroom and came up with nothing.

The leader turned to his partner. "You smell something, Fraley?"

"Yeah, Lieutenant. Exhaust fumes. We better check the garage."

The four officers moved in unison from the bedroom, past the living room and into the kitchen. By the time they reached the inside garage door, the smell of carbon monoxide was overpowering.

The Lieutenant motioned to his team. "We've got a running car in the garage, could be a suicide. But we'll treat it as an active threat. Weapons ready? Let's go."

The men rushed through the door, found an idling sedan, but no physical danger. Fraley reached through the open window and turned the ignition off. Another officer lifted the garage door to disseminate the carbon monoxide.

The Lieutenant opened the car door and a body lay in the seat, unresponsive and apparently dead. A check of the carotid artery confirmed the obvious. Fraley pulled the driver's license from the vic's pocket and verified the picture. "Name's Allen Costas. He's wanted for a double homicide back in Amarillo, Texas."

"Looks like we got our man." The Lieutenant took the sunglasses and headphones off the dead man. "What the hell is this stuff? Some kinda new age shit to die by?" The Lieutenant stroked his chin. "This whole scene doesn't feel right. It's too coincidental. A guy named Slash in Amarillo, Texas passes a tip on Costas' location. Marco Island PD gets a call. We show up, and the suspect's just committed suicide." He ran a hand through his hair and turned toward Fraley. "Something's not right."

"Want to call Amarillo?"

"Yeah, have them send a detective to interview the tipster. See what they can shake out of him."

Fraley made the call and informed the Amarillo detective of the situation at Costas' residence, as well as their interest in Slash. The Florida Lieutenant listened in as the detective stated that an explosion and shooting had just been called in at Slash's residence. A team was on the way and the details were sketchy.

The Lieutenant and Fraley exchanged glances. "Get

CSI out here, Fraley. I want a closer look at the body. My gut says we're missing something important."

35

OH, HELL YES

I LOOK UP INTO DR. NAVARRO'S eyes and see a glimmer
of the person I used to know. It's not much, but I might
work it to my advantage. Then, his eyes move to the left
and I see a shift in his persona. A dark and disturbing
ember ignites. Something suggests that I might not be
exploiting our relationship after all, and that possibility
sets my heart pounding.

The doctor offers me a vague smile. "I just want to
know how to stop time. Once we have the secret, you'll be
free to go."

I remember the muzzle flash on my bare arms back at
Slash's apartment, and think of the man I loved, the one
who brought a smile when I was down, the one who gave
me hope after my parent's deaths, the one who gave me a
reason to live.

"Navarro, I thought you were my friend, I trusted you!
But you killed Slash, you sorry bastard. Why should I help
you?" I grip the chair's armrests, flex my muscles. "Tell me.
Why the *hell* should I help you? You can go fuck yourself!"

"Your parents died a pointless and tragic death, and
now you've lost your boyfriend. You have no one. But if
you agree to our demand, then you will live. You can start

over with another life. I don't think you're ready to die. Are you?"

The thought catches me in the gut. With the loss of my parents and Slash, do I really have a reason to live?

Navarro leans forward, blocks Father Muerte's view, and mouths the words, "Things aren't as they appear. Just trust me."

The doctor backs away. For a moment I am genuinely surprised. Can I really trust him? The answer echoes in my mind—do I have a choice? I look around and see rusted industrial equipment, pools of stagnant water, old cigarette butts and graffiti on the concrete walls. My thoughts turn to Slash, and I think, what would he do?

Live. Slash would choose to fight and live.

I tamp my fear down and shift my gaze to Father Muerte. "What assurance do I have that you'll keep your word? You play by a different set of rules and I don't trust you."

Father Muerte replies, "Doctor Navarro will give you three very good reasons to comply."

The doctor removes his cell phone, puts it in my face, and cues up a video. When he presses play, there are three, very large, feral hogs in a small outdoor pen. In the video, Father Muerte is standing on the bottom rail and throws dismembered human parts into the center of the pen. The feeding frenzy is sickening, and I turn my head away. "You've made your point." But I can't help myself. "Shithead."

"Now, tell me how it's done." Father Muerte smirks.

I shudder because I have no choice. "You have to take a thirty-minute immersion pill and use Dr. Navarro's induction device for it to work. Then concentrate on travelling to the heart of time."

"That's all?" Navarro holds a knife to my throat, and I remain motionless. "You see, I don't trust you either."

"Then, you go through a door, and tell the time-keeper

where you want to go. When he takes you there, time will be stopped."

Father Muerte nods to the doctor, who lowers his knife. "How many pills do you have?"

"Two."

"Good, because you're going with me." Father Muerte pulls up another chair and places it next to mine. He leans in close, runs his tongue up my neck and licks my ear. "Where are the drugs?"

I am beyond disgusted but keep my temper in check. "In my pants pocket."

Dr. Navarro removes the pill bottle, opens it and taps out the last two doses. One of which he gives to Father Muerte, and the other he places between his forefinger and thumb.

"Set the pill under your tongue and put on Navarro's sunglasses and headphones, then hit the power button. After a few minutes, you will be aware of an immense darkness. It's critical that you concentrate totally on the word, *Naraka*, which is the ancient term for heart of time."

Father Muerte nods to the doctor, and he puts his two fingers and the pill under my tongue. After he removes them, I sit back in my chair and wait. With Navarro's help, Father Muerte engages the doctor's induction device. "When I'm under, put the gear on Archer and start her immersion."

Navarro waits. His brow furrows. His breathing becomes labored and intense.

About ten minutes in, Father Muerte is fully immersed and immobilized. I look up at Dr. Navarro. The corners of his eyes crinkle in mirth. He holds up the palmed immersion pill meant for me.

"Great save, Doctor. I didn't know if you were receptive to telepathic thoughts, but you came through just like I wanted you to."

"I'm the worst with ESP. Never had it, never will. But I realized you had an opening when Father Muerte proposed that both of you do an immersion. When you said, 'things will go black,' I improvised and kept your pill hidden from view, knowing that he would lose consciousness after he took his dose." Dr. Navarro pulls his knife back out and begins to cut at the duct tape on my left forearm. "I didn't kill Slash, Archer. He's still alive." Navarro looks up at me as he confesses. "When we were back at his house, I knocked him out with a blow to the jaw, then fired my gun into the floor. Father Muerte was outside and had to believe I was following his instructions."

A terrible weight lifts from my mind. I breathe a sigh of relief. "Thank you for sparing Slash's life. How are you involved in all this and why are you helping me?"

"I was pulled into this mess by Le Cadavre, who later turned me over to Father Muerte, who in turn, dosed me with a mind-control drug. The reason I'm helping you is because you're a good person, you've done nothing to deserve this punishment. The evil needs to be stopped.

Father Muerte has a severe psychiatric disorder, in which he identifies with death, while assuming an emotionless demeanor. Under this façade is a psyche harboring atrocious acts of violence. Since a public appearance by him would be disastrous, he picks his students to do his dirty work by dosing them with a mind-control drug that fosters intense feelings of love for him. Once you experience this bond, you will do anything for him, including murder."

"How long does the bonding last?'

"Three days. On my first two, Father Muerte submitted me to extreme psychological duress, after which I developed an intense bond with him. Because of the deep imprint the inflicted horror had upon me, he said that I will sporadically blank out on the third day and inflict evil upon those whom he has chosen."

I just purchased a ticket to Stephen King's lottery of dark horror, and I'm in line to win first prize.

"Archer, you've got to get away from me before the darkness takes over."

Now I must worry about getting away before the darkness takes over? "Can you hurry with the knife? Please?"

Dr. Navarro is about one inch into my left binding, when he stops. The kindness drains out of his eyes and is replaced by a dark pit of smoldering rage. I struggle against the cut tape, jerk with all my strength, but it only rips a quarter of an inch. There is another foot of tape left and things don't look good.

He looks up at me. "Daddy says mommy has been bad. *Real* bad."

The doctor's voice is whiny and petulant, like that of a five-year-old child. A deranged, five- year-old with a very sharp knife.

And no one knows where I am.

36

JUST FIND ME, DAMN IT

"SIR, ARE YOU AWAKE?" SLASH'S BODY moved as someone hovered over him, prodding his shoulder with a vigorous push. But it was the vial of ammonia under his nose that really pissed him off.

"Yes, God damn it. I am fucking awake. Now, get that shit out of my face." Slash pushed the ampoule away, and it took him a few seconds to orient himself. His vision was clearing, his ears rung like the inside of a Sunday church bell, and his sucker-punched jaw throbbed unmercifully. Other than that, he was all right.

The officer dropped the ammonia. "Who detonated the flash bang, and was anyone else in the room with you when it happened?"

"Archer?" Slash pushed himself up from the floor. He scrambled to the other side of the bed. Nothing. A mad dash to the bathroom. Still nothing. Out into the living room.

Absolutely. Nothing.

Slash ran his hands down his face and slumped onto the couch. He answered the officer's question with a sense of dread, knowing that voicing the truth would only give it power. "Her name is Archer Ann Wilson, and she's gone. We were in here together when the flash-bang went off, and whoever punched me, took her."

"Do you know who might have kidnapped her?"

Something hovered just below Slash's consciousness, threatening to yield a bounty of information. But it was stuck on a mental disconnect, thanks to the concussive force of a well-placed flash-bang and the dislocating force of a powerful punch. He pinched his eyes shut, forced himself to think. Archer's life depended on it.

Slash's phone rang once, and he ripped it from his pocket. It was not Archer, but the ringing reminded him of something critical. He and Archer had installed a personal GPS tracking app a year ago on their phones, enabling them to locate each other throughout the day. Slash engaged the program and a pulsing blue dot appeared on a map grid, revealing her location.

He had minutes to get to Archer. To save her. If he didn't find her in time, his life would be over. "I don't know who has Archer, but I know where she is. Let's get our asses in gear. Cause I have a need for speed."

37

"MOMMY'S BEEN BAD." THE DOCTOR STABBED the air between Archer and himself with a filet knife. "And you know what that means."

I ignore the obvious threat because I have only one chance to get it right. "What's your name, honey?"

He looks at me suspiciously. "Manuel."

"That's a sweet name. Who's your daddy?"

"Him." He points toward Father Muerte.

"Looks like daddy's taking a nap." I yawn. "Would you like to take one, too?"

Manuel leans toward me and places the blade against my cheek. "Daddy says big boys don't need naps."

"I forgot." I ignore the steel pressing into my flesh and motion with my head toward daddy. "He's been sleeping for a while now. Why don't you cut me loose so I can help him take his pill?"

Concern wrinkles Manuel's brow. He reaches over and shakes daddy's knee.

My heart rides up my throat as he attempts to rouse Father Muerte. "Can you see the bottle in his hand? It's time for his medicine."

Manuel looks over. "Yes. I see. Is it really time?"

"It is."

"I don't know if Daddy would like that."

"If he doesn't take his medicine, he could die. You don't want him to die, do you?"

"Daddy not die." He moves the filet knife between my left forearm and the chair's arm, slicing six inches of tape away.

My heart spikes painfully in my chest. Hurry, I silently urge. Hurry before it's too late. The man-child cuts a few more inches. I scream inside, you're taking too much time.

He stops and glares at me. I see the rising anger. "You're trying to trick me. Daddy doesn't take pills."

"I'm your mommy, Manuel. I wouldn't lie to you." I tug at my restraints and try to free myself.

"You did lie. You did." Manuel raises the knife high. "That's a no-no."

Then he plunges the blade downward with all his force.

38

JOHN WHO?

SLASH AND THE OFFICER WERE A half mile from Archer's location when the unthinkable happened. The policeman removed his handcuffs and passed them to Slash. "Cuff your right wrist and fasten the other end on the floor ring by your feet."

"Why the hell are you doing this?" Slash slammed the dash. "You'll need some help in there."

"Backup's on the way, and I don't need a civilian John Wayne in the way."

The officer muttered something and turned to Slash, "Do it now." Both the severe tone of the barked order and the hard lines on the officer's face said he meant it.

Reluctantly, he cuffed himself as instructed. "You don't know what you're getting into."

"Don't worry, when backup gets here, we'll have the advantage as we go in." The policeman checked Slash's locator map as he drove across the abandoned lot. A rusted, steel building stood on the back side. Parking his cruiser beside an empty car, he opened his door. "Looks like this is it. We'll have her out in a few minutes."

The officer exited his vehicle, and Slash tugged at his cuffs. "God damn it, you need me. You don't know these people. They're killers."

"THAT'S WHY I GET PAID THE big…." The young police-man was cut off by a loud, piercing, scream, coming from inside the metal building. He immediately drew his gun and approached the structure, ignoring Slash's curses, ig-noring his better judgment, and ignoring the small, inner voice that said, you don't want to die today.

THE OFFICER ENTERED THE BUILDING WITH his gun drawn, and Slash jerked against his cuffs, screamed in frustration, felt the blood run down his hand.

He had to get out of the restraints. He had to get to Archer before it was too late. He had to find a key. So, he ripped the officer's clip board off the dash. Yanked a cup of pens from a drink holder and emptied it on the floor. Slash tore the glove box open. Inside was a handcuff key, a nine-millimeter automatic, and an extra ammo clip.

Finally. The jackpot!

39

YOU'RE CUTTING IT CLOSE

MANUEL/NAVARRO PLUNGES THE BLADE DOWNWARD with all his force, and I judge the trajectory of the blade, rock back in the wooden chair, and spread my upper legs wide. The razor-sharp knife slices the fabric on my inner left thigh, leaves a gaping hole in my denim jeans, and a thin, superficial cut three inches long.

The blade slams into the solid wood seat, next to my crotch, and breaks off at the handle. My scream echoes off the rusty, metal walls only to die uncomfortably in the oppressive room.

I gasp for air, and cannot breathe, I stare, but cannot see. I tremble and cannot stop.

"Manuel, you need to let me go. The police are on their way."

Hopeless despair washes over me and the reality that I will probably die sinks in. The kind and considerate Dr. Navarro isn't strong enough to push through his alternate self. I have used every trick I can think of and nothing has worked long enough to get free. I tug at my restraints and feel my strength ebb away.

He cocks his head. "I protect daddy now." Manuel reaches into his pants pocket and removes a small revolver.

He points it at my head, thumbs back the hammer. "Reach for the sky, Pilgrim."

The absurdity of his statement hits me hard. This isn't something a five-year-old would say. It is something an adult might say. I carefully weigh my next few words. "Manuel, will you let Doctor Navarro come out?"

There is a flash in the man-child's eyes that lets me know Navarro is in there. Manuel still points a gun at my head, and I notice a slight tremor in his hand, which turns to a shake, then a cautious lowering of the revolver.

"That's great honey, you're such a good boy." The weapon now hangs by his side, his trigger finger unengaged. The air crackles from a release of psychic tension as Dr. Navarro returns.

His face twists in horror as he takes it in—the broken blade lying against my crotch, the sliced fabric, the oozing cut on my upper thigh, and the realization that he caused it all. His eyes fill with tears as he struggles to comprehend, to beg forgiveness, to make it right.

Just as he starts to speak, a man screams, "Police! Put the weapon down." The young officer approaches from around a rusted boiler with gun drawn.

The doctor's eyes shift and the man-child, Manuel re-emerges. His forefinger moves toward the trigger and his laser pointer dots the center of the officer's forehead.

Shit!

My last chance at freedom evaporates before my eyes.

Manuel's high-pitched voice squeals in anger.

Two shots ring out and I scream again.

Then quietness assaults my senses with a velvet thunder.

40

COME OUT, COME OUT, WHERE VER YOU ARE

SLASH RUSHED INTO THE STEEL BUILDING, gun drawn, and ran around the rusted machinery to see what he feared most. The officer was dead with a bullet wound to his head. Archer was tied to a chair, head down and slumped against her restraints. Slash had heard two shots fired and couldn't tell if she was unharmed, wounded, or dead. Standing above Archer was a tall, Hispanic male, holding a revolver against her temple.

Slash leveled his weapon. "Put the gun down, or I'll blow your head off."

"Manuel, tell you once. Archer dies if you don't put yours down."

A cloud of spent gunpowder filled the room. A rat scurried somewhere in the shadows. A very rattled Slash swallowed painfully. "Just put the gun down and we'll all be cool." Until he could determine if Archer were all right, he had to be calm. Slash made eye contact with the gunman and swung around to Archer. "Arch, you okay?"

No response.

Then, a little louder, "Archer?"

The man-child motioned with the butt of his gun. "She screams and it scares me. So, I hit her hard. I hit her in the head." Manuel motioned with his gun and Slash saw Archer's blood on the base of the grip.

Manuel put the gun against Archer's head. "Mommy's been bad. Daddy says she has to die."

A groggy Archer regained consciousness and looked up at Slash. Her life hung in the balance. But, when Slash saw her mouth, 'back off,' he knew she had a plan.

"Doctor Navarro?"

Manuel's eyes widened.

"Doctor Navarro, this is Archer and I'm speaking to you. You must regain control. There can be no more bloodshed. Too many have already died. The child, Manuel, has to be stopped right now."

Archer forced a smile. "You said that the mind control drug lasts for three days, and you're within hours of its ending. Stop this madness, get control of the child."

"Daddy says mommy has to die. We always do what daddy says."

The doctor's face twisted from the mental effort as he finally wrestled control from Manuel. "Archer, I don't know how long I can hold Manuel back. He's too strong. You need to leave. Right now."

Slash took his knife out and cut Archer's bindings. He picked her up from the chair and quickly carried her out of the building. Enveloped by the cool morning air, they heard the wail of sirens and turned to see the first of three patrol cars rush into the parking area.

The sergeant got out and recognized Slash from earlier. "Where is your escort?"

"He's inside. Dead. The man who killed him is in there," Slash pointed toward the steel building. "He has a gun."

The muscles in the sergeant's jaw clenched and a dark look came into his eyes. As lead officer, his men bunched around him waiting for an entrance plan.

A gunshot from inside simplified their entry.

I SIT IN THE BACK OF the ambulance after having my thigh wound looked at. Mostly a scratch, but the gash on my temple took a little more attention from my gung-ho paramedic. Slash and I watch the two bodies being brought out on separate gurneys and loaded into the morgue vans. It was a shame the young officer had to die, as well as my friend, Dr. Navarro. I owe a debt of gratitude to the doctor, though. He kept the murderous Manuel at bay long enough for Slash and me to escape. Unfortunately, the doctor committed suicide to end the terror. He was so close to outlasting the drug's effects—so damned close to overcoming his alternate self. He gave his life so I could live, and I will forever hold him close to my heart.

I tell Slash about Father Muerte and his indoctrination of the Dr., and it is with a dose of pleasure that I watch the flesh-colored madman being led out of the rusty steel building in a straitjacket.

Slash leans in toward me. "Any idea how he went looney tunes?"

"Officially, no. Unofficially... how's your knowledge of Buddhist terminology?"

"Not as good as yours, so go ahead."

"I told Father Muerte that in order to get to the heart of time, all he had to do was concentrate on the term, *Naraka.*"

"Since he came out in a straitjacket, I'll hazard a guess he didn't make it to the heart of time."

"Not a bad observation for a stoner." I grin.

My boyfriend rubs his hands on his pants. "So, do you care to share?"

"Only if you take me out for drinks and dinner."

"Oh, you wicked woman. All right, tell me."

"Well, *Naraka* isn't the definition for the heart of time, as you now know. But it is the Buddhist term for what we call Hell."

Slash whistles appreciatively. "Remind me to never piss you off, Arch. I'm sure that Father Muerte's brain is scrambled after his immersion, and I never had this conversation with you."

"What conversation?" I punch him on the arm.

Slash moves in to kiss me, but we're interrupted by his ringing cell phone.

He looks at the caller ID. "It's Marco Island, PD."

Over the next half hour, I listen to the speaker phone as the Marco Island Lieutenant grills Slash over how he got Costas's address. Slash answers truthfully, even refers the officer to contact his new supervisor in charge of the up and running psychic espionage program—featuring Slash and I as lead participants.

Before Slash disconnects, I have a question about Costas that was raised when I did my immersion and located him last night. I take the phone. "Lieutenant, by any chance did you find a medicine bottle in Costas possession?"

Stony silence, then, he coughs. *"Yes, I did."*

"And was the label blank, except for one word?"

"Yes, it was."

Sweat pops out on my brow. "What did it say?"

"Indefinite."

That is what I saw when I made my trip to Costas' house. It was a pill bottle on the breakfast table. A bottle labeled indefinite. With a pill inside that allowed him to live after committing suicide. Allowed him to dupe the police. Allowed his consciousness, and Le Cadavre's, to live. In an innocent host's body

They are not dead.
And because of that, I will surely die.
Unless... I find them first.

41

PEEK-A-BOO, I SEE YOU

IT HAS BEEN TWO WEEKS SINCE Dr. Navarro died and Father Muerte was committed to a psychiatric facility. I still grieve the loss of the doctor, but because of his selfless action, I'm still alive.

During this time, Slash and I have been working with Jason Bir, the new psychic espionage director by developing a protocol that protects the psychic operators from undue control by the director.

Jason Bir, who is the physical opposite of Costas, stands six feet tall, is slender, and has a genuine look of compassion upon his face. He gives me a thumbs-up for the first launch of the program. "Are you ready Archer?"

I give him a nod and am glad he's fresh blood in a project plagued by corrupt leadership, namely Allen Costas and his enforcer, Le Cadavre. Both men are physically dead, however, their consciousness thrives in host bodies from alternate realities to our physical world. The two criminals move around, a lot, and I've been following their financial trail for weeks.

It's like when you have an infestation of rats, you put out the bait and hope they take it.

Only, I'm the bait. I take an immersion pill and put on

the glasses and earphones as I lie on the room's couch. Jason sits patiently next to me and concentrates on my destination. As do I.

My mission is to psychically probe a known contact of Costas. A former stripper, called Candy Cain, whose name came up on our facilities hot sheet of suspicious associates. Twenty million dollars has passed through her hands on the way out of the country. It takes a whole lot of lap dances to amass that kind of money, so Candy must be a conduit for Costas' cash—cash that has probably been amassed by stealing America's covert secrets.

I focus on entering Candy's mind and look through her eyes to see a very naked, very aroused, very aggressive man lying on top of her. His hands are around her neck and squeeze tight.

Candy gasps for air. "Yea, baby. Take me to the edge!"

He grunts and thrusts hard inside her. She is on the edge of a massive orgasm and moves her hips to meet his.

With both hands firmly around her throat, he squeezes harder. His left thumb searches for the beat of her carotid artery.

The young stripper arches her back and is unable to move because her hands and legs are tied to the bedposts. Candy is into autoerotic asphyxia, a highly dangerous, restriction of air for the purpose of sexual arousal. Or more crudely, she craves the feeling of coming and going at the same time.

I look through Candy's eyes at the man who chokes the life from her. My heart goes out to this woman as he crushes her throat. Candy's oxygen-starved body bucks into overdrive. I feel her heart beating wildly in her chest as it bumps and thumps her upper torso. He continues to thrust savagely, with abandoned fury, deep and feral.

Candy focuses on the beginning of a Hiroshima-grade

'O.' Her hips pump harder, and her lungs scream for oxygen. The mother of all orgasms unfolds inside her. The intensity of Candy's emotions overwhelms me, and I am sickened by this whole scenario. How can a sane person desire sexual satisfaction through asphyxiation?

Her partner is relentless. Chokes the life from her. Slams against her again and again.

Her hips thrust against his, and a ball of sexual energy moves up her stomach, across her chest, and into her brain. A hurricane of sexual release explodes in a cataclysmic discharge. Her toes curl, her fists clench, her body shudders.

She experiences the most earth-shaking moment of her life.

And is in the process of dying, as well.

Her partner refuses to release his grip, then presses his thumb against her carotid artery. Candy arches her body, trying to stop the choking, thrashes her legs to dislodge her partner. Darkness descends quickly, and the last words Candy hears are, "It's not every day you can kill two bitches with one stone." Laughter rumbles in her partner's throat, "Archer, you fell for my trap. You came to me just like I anticipated."

Candy's life spirals downward, dying at the hands of a Costas controlled puppet. I frantically consider, *if the host dies, do I die too?* I am unsure. Candy's heart goes into atrial fibrillation, and I don't have a choice. Either die. Or make a radical decision. With only seconds to spare, I leave Candy's body and psychically will the words, time, time, time to deliver me to the realm of time.

I just hope it's not too late.

42

IT'S MELTING TIME

I NARROWLY ESCAPE DEATH AT THE hands of a Costas controlled marionette. My heart thuds against my ribs, and I never want to be that close to dying again. Everything in me shouts to be careful. But where have I landed?

I find myself in a room full of clocks. Grandfather clocks, wall clocks, alarm clocks.

All manner of clocks.

There are clocks on the walls, clocks on the floor, and as I look up, there are clocks on the ceiling.

I have gone from nearly dying, to the freakin' bizarre. The entire room pulses with the essence of time—the veiled beat that lies behind every object, place, and person in our world. The same vibration that drives reality forward, from beginning to end. The vibration that is present in all human endeavors, from start to finish. And the same vibration that lies behind the fabric of our lives, intertwined, yet unnoticed, until our time comes to an end.

From birth to death, the vibration is undetectable. Yet, here in the annex of time, its presence is massive. Its heartbeat pounds out a staggering force that vibrates my scalp down to my toes. My very soul moves while my breath is purged by the pressure upon my chest.

Then, the unthinkable happens. The room of clocks goes silent. There is no clicking, no ticking, no vibration.

Nothing at all.

It's as if the womb of time has aborted all trace of life. Swept its presence away and left a barren room in its place.

The pit of my stomach lurches and the sudden silence screams inside my head. I look upon the staggering number of silent clocks and grieve the absence of time.

Of movement.

Of *life*.

A circular wall clock in front of me ruptures its lower boundary. Like a melting Dali timepiece in the Persistence of Memory painting. The bottom of the frame births a large, bucket-sized drop, full of liquid chrome, plastic, metal, and glass. It separates from the larger clock, rolls down the wall, and puddles on the floor.

The fallen mass begins to flatten. Reconstructs itself and morphs into a smaller, rigid, circumference. Rising through the shiny liquid within the clock's frame, the numbers, one through twelve float into sight and are followed by the rapid formation of the clock's hands.

Suddenly, three falling drops splatter around me. I look up and see the clocks on the ceiling beginning to melt, sending composite droplets down around me. The smaller globules of liquid time look like bulbous, oily splotches with traces of crystal highlights. They form into small, pentagon-shaped time pieces, and reveal dial numbers in a random manner. A four is followed by a one with no logical sequence to their circular progression. As I pocket these three Daliesque aberrations, an intuitive hunch evolves within my mind that these three timepieces have been placed in my path for a reason.

If this is my path, has my presence here caused this anomaly? Have I disrupted time?

What the shit have I done?

I can't help but wonder, will I be able to get out of here?

Or will I be stuck in a place where time has vanished?

If I do escape, what waits for me at home?

43

SOMETHING BAD IS COMING

THE FIRST THING I SEE WHEN I awaken in another world is an alternate Costas leaning over me. He's frozen in place and looking down with his mouth open, apparently in mid-sentence. I ease off his couch and move around the office. Judging by the sun blazing through his window, it's mid-afternoon. A quick look in the wall mirror and I'm bludgeoned with shock. I expected to see my astral body.

But it's not, it's the real me.

I glance down at my right hand and affirm my missing finger. What the devil is going on? And what just occurred?

Something bad is happening. My consciousness has moved from one world to another, and my actual body is manifested in Costas' office, where time is stopped. I have a sudden craving for an ice cold Yoo-hoo. The former director, in my original world, kept a stash in the mini fridge beside his desk. I bend over for a quick look, grab one, and hear something clink in my left pocket.

With more pressing matters than checking out a random noise, I open a bottle labeled, Yee- haw. And can't help but marvel over the slight name divergence between my world and this one. After a soul-satisfying slug of chocolaty, sugary, caffeinated, pseudo beverage, I reach into my jean's pocket and pull out three small timepieces, the source of the noise.

The presence of these watches poses a problem—how did they get from the annex of time into an alternate world? How did my body get here, too? I thought that only human consciousness and astral bodies could travel between worlds. I knock back another ice-cold gulp of Yee-haw. Study the three pieces of irrefutable proof in my other hand.

The watch's bases are all pentagon-shaped, about one-half inch thick, and contain a grey, oily solution under a glass dial cover. The watch numbers, which were earlier in a random order, begin to present themselves in proper numerical sequence. The movement appears synchronized as all three watches reflect the same progression. Also, a second, minute, and hour hand start to form.

I look into my subconscious. Intuitively know that time is starting up again.

I stare at the three mysterious watches. Wonder, what the hell have I gotten into?

My gut tells me these clocks represent more than I ever dreamed of.

I focus on the doorway to the Time Guardian's home. Pray that I get there.

In time.

44

THE PORTAL KEY

I EMERGE FROM DARKNESS AND FIND myself in the apartment above Time. The fact that my immersion is open-ended suggests some serious problems. Over one hour ago, I started in the psychic espionage director, Jason Bir's, room, then experienced the sexual strangulation of Candy Cain. Next, I found myself in the annex of time, and after that, my physical body popped in on an alternate Costas at his office. Finally, I've stopped in the Time Guardian's apartment, and gratefully no one is here to kill me. I sense a guiding force behind my four immersion stops and hope the beast that has driven me to this point is about to be tamed.

As I look around the apartment, I'm greeted with the same overflowing ashtrays, same natty carpet, and same crusty bong.

Mr. Ed, who's in his early twenties, is tall, has a muscular build, and black, wavy hair. When he's not in classes, he has a gig as the keeper of time and dimensional order. One of his jobs is to lead the various visitors down the Hallway of Infinity to their destination of choice.

He acknowledges my stare and crosses his eyes to emphasize that he's smoking some primo shit. One finger goes up in the air for me to wait. Seeds pop in his bowl as he inhales the last bit of his hit. Then the seated Time Guardian places the bong to the side and exhales.

The young man smiles. "When things were disrupted downstairs in the annex, I knew you'd be here soon. Figured I'd have time for a smoke." He situates his hands in his lap, sits back in his chair, steeples his fingers. "Seems like the annex of time started to, for want of a better term, melt. Dali could have gotten his inspiration from the mess down there."

"It's one thing to break a dish or a leg, but how the hell have I broken time?"

"Not to worry, Archer."

"What do you mean?"

The Time Guardian leans forward in his chair. "You didn't create the meltdown. It was started by the rider, yesterday morning."

"Whoa, if I didn't cause it, then who or what is a rider?"

He cracks his knuckles. "Well, a rider is a dominant consciousness who directs a weaker-willed person to do his bidding."

I'm beginning to get the picture, now. "Would the rider's name be…."

"Costas."

"Dear God, Ed. He must have figured out a way to project his host's astral body. When you met him yesterday morning, what did he do?" I expect the worst.

"He brought me a bunch of this kick-ass weed, which I immediately smoked."

I sigh, push my hair back and lean forward. "What happened after that?"

"I answered his questions, then developed a bad case of the munchies. Told Costas, thanks. Went down the Hallway of Infinity, stopped at my favorite Italian restaurant, and ate two Hero sandwiches."

"What did Costas want?"

Mr. Ed's eyebrows furrow and form a slight V. "He asked me take him to the door of an alternate world's Federal gold repository."

"Oh my God!" Panic rips down my spine. "And you took him?"

"I didn't have a choice." He turns both palms upward.

"What do you mean you didn't have a choice? It's obvious he was going to steal the bullion."

"I knew it, and he knew it. But when the great Architect created the multiverse, he also gave mankind the gift of free will."

"Meaning?" My heart pounds a rhythm of fear.

"Unless there is immediate harm to the dimensional system, and I mean in the next few minutes, I have to follow his requests."

"Requests as in plural?"

"Yes," he spreads his hands. "Costas has breached three alternate worlds in a different way—physically, mentally, and spiritually. In the physical sense, he formed a bridge between that world's gold repository and a secure location on your planet Earth. And is about finished looting their wealth as we speak."

"How can Costas be taking the gold now? I was nearly killed by him an hour ago."

The Time Guardian lowers his voice, "Costas has figured out how to control the weak-willed with just his mind. His workers are moving the gold through the portal to a haven in Costas's home world. If the situation escalates, the Architect has one safeguard in place—a last resort solution to protect dimensional integrity."

I think about that for a few seconds, rock back on my heels. This shit with Costas has gone on long enough. It must stop, right now.

"Is there any relation to the failing of time here and the breach he created?" I glance at Mr. Ed.

"Most definitely. When you link two different worlds with a portal, you open them up for a meltdown. Each reality has a different gravitational signature. That will cause a disruption if they ever get in close proximity. Instead of the worlds attracting each other, they will be repulsed, and the foundation of time is the first to suffer. Unless the portal is closed, and soon, the damage will be monumental."

"Holy shit!"

Mr. Ed motions to the three watches in my hand. "Time itself is a living entity and when its' foundation was attacked, it formed the three keys you hold."

"What do you mean?" This is like something out of Harry Potter.

"I mean that each of the watches is a key to close the portals that Costas has activated."

For the first time, it appears that I can do something to stop him. With a little spit and determination, I can get ahead of the bastard.

I look the man directly in the eye. "It seems counter-productive that Costas would engage a meltdown in the world where he's storing the gold."

"It's not what you think, Archer. You see, he knew that you would be looking for him, and he's counted on you to stop the disaster before it happens. You have loved ones in your world?"

"Yes,"

"He knows that, and is using it to his advantage, because you always do the right thing."

I gnaw thoughtfully on my lower lip, because Costas is spot-on with his assessment. "How much time do I have before the meltdown?"

"Look at the watch that's running backwards."

A quick glance and I find it. "The time says, 11:58 a.m. And how much is left?"

"Two minutes are already gone. That leaves you eight minutes to save your world."

Rage blossoms in my mind. I plant my feet wide apart. Feel my lips pull back to expose my teeth. "Costas killed my parents. He will *not* kill my boyfriend. So, tell me how to use the key, and get the hell out of my way!"

45

T-MINUS 4 MINUTES
AND COUNTING

MR. ED JUMPS UP FROM HIS chair, grabs hold of my hand, and jerks me toward a door leading out of the living room. We run through the threshold, into a darkened hallway, and are greeted with the glare of overhead lights that flicker on, one after the other. They continue onward and narrow to a smudge of brightness, seemingly light years ahead of us. On either side of the fluorescent bulbs are countless doors which batter me with the visual intensity of the infinite.

We keep running down the corridor until my guide stops, bends over to catch his breath, and points at the doorknob on his left.

"I think this is the room Costas entered." He gasps until he gets his wind back.

With a glance at the countdown watch, I push past Mr. Ed and open the door. The stench of burning sulfur abrades my nostrils as I teeter at the edge of a pit of screaming souls. I can hear the pop and sizzle of burning flesh and feel fire licking at my feet

But the pot smoking Time Guardian grabs my arm and yanks me to safety.

I purge the sulfurous smell by sneezing, then glare at

Mr. Ed. "I thought you knew where we were going. What was that place?"

"Do you remember the other day when you told Father Muerte to concentrate on *Naraka?*"

"Yes." Then the obvious hits me. "Don't tell me, that was hell?"

"Your own intimate slice, up close and personal," Mr. Ed narrows his eyes. "In the Hallway of Infinity, if you can visualize and think of your destination, you can go anywhere."

"What's the possibility that you'll think of the correct door Costas went through?" I try to keep the anger from my voice. No need to piss off the guide when you really need one, even if he's higher than a kite.

Mr. Ed hangs his head in shame. "Sorry. Next time I'll lay off the bong."

Obviously, he realizes he screwed up, and I accept his apology. He steps to the next door and gives a hand flourish with a bow, "This one is what you're looking for."

I look at the watch. Four minutes left. My brain screams to hurry. The stress causes my fingers and toes to tingle, so I close my eyes and think.

Okay, Archer. Grip the doorknob. Take a deep breath.

Jerk the door open.

Holy *shit!*

46

FOLLOW THE GOLD BRICK ROAD

THE BREATH CATCHES IN MY THROAT as I gape in silence at the mass of wealth in front of me. There are fifteen or twenty, fifty-gallon drums of South African Krugerrands, American Gold Eagles, and Chinese Panda coins.

I'm also stunned, amazed, and shocked at the gold bars stacked on the floor. They cover a sixty by one-hundred feet area and sit on a concrete pad inside a nondescript metal building. I recognize the 12.4-kilogram bar as the one preferred by traders and investors.

And there must be fifteen to twenty thousand of them stacked in neat, square piles. I run my finger over one bar and realize there is some mondo wealth here, but I don't have time to appreciate it. My job is to place the watch key in the portal receptacle and sever the connection between two different worlds. Hopefully, before they self-destruct.

I turn around and face the empty, depository vault. The massive, reinforced door is wide open and inside is a vast, barren floor, with dozens of bare pallets that once held the gold bars.

The object of my interest is the round segment that connects these two worlds. It's about seven feet in the middle, pulses with a greenish hue, and is smooth to the touch.

My mouth is dry, and I try to summon some moisture as I take a quick look at the watch. It's less than two minutes to insert the key and stop the imminent destruction. I am glad I don't have to worry about resistance from Costas's gold movers because he wants me to stop the destruction as much as I do. What good would the wealth do him if it's destroyed?

Only ninety seconds left, and the possibility of pulverization presses closer.

I wipe the sweat from my forehead and remember our sprint down the Hallway of Infinity to the door where Mr. Ed thought Costas had gone earlier. I nearly ended up in a burning hell, all because the Time Guardian was stoned.

He promised that the keyhole would be exactly dead center at the bottom of the connection. Fear churns my stomach. What if he's wrong, again? There will be no second chances for me to get this done. This is it. Everything—my life, my world, depends on getting it right.

I move to the center of the portal with a barren vault behind me and a gorged, gold packed, stash of stolen swag in front of me. I go over every inch of the bottom half of the foot- wide connection and find nothing. Time is ticking away, and I don't like this at all. My eyes blink and sweat runs down my spine as I trace my fingers up the top half.

There's still nothing.

So, where the hell is it? My head begins to throb and a sharp pain shoots across my temples. I've come so far and can't fail now.

I look down where Mr. Ed said the receptacle would be. Then, I look straight up. And see a pentagon-shaped opening above my head.

Rising on my toes, I'm inches shy of reaching the hole, and I don't have the strength to drag a massive pallet over to stand on.

I'm four inches too short. But I'm not beaten. Not yet.

With thirty seconds left, I jump up. Try to slap the key in the opening. It bangs against the edges, misses slightly.

Twenty seconds remain.

I spring again and almost insert it.

Fifteen seconds, and it's all up to me.

Adrenaline spikes my nervous system.

Another leap, another miss. My heart pounds a frantic rhythm and my leg muscles tense.

Eight seconds left.

I stand in the center of the portal, stare up at the hole, and concentrate on the shape of the watch in my hand.

In my mind, I see the two coming together.

Four seconds.

I jump. Reach out, hoping….

One second remains.

And the key slams into the hole.

A blast of pressure closes a shield between the two worlds and severs the connection. I sink weakly to the floor, my legs unable to support me.

There are two more portals to close—and only thirty minutes to do it.

47

CLOSE YOUR EYES,
HANG ON TIGHT

I OPEN MY EYES AND JERK up from the couch in Jason Bir's office. Slash stands beside him and their faces are a study of mixed emotions—surprise and fear.

Jason, the new director of psychic espionage, looks at his watch, his lips a compressed white line. "Archer, you were gone for over an hour."

I acknowledge Jason with a quick, "I know." Then I reach over and kiss Slash. "I thought I'd never see you again."

He hugs me tight and whispers in my ear, "You don't know how many gray hairs you've given me, babe."

"I love you."

"Same. Wanna tell us why you were gone for an hour?"

I quickly fill them in on my immersion, starting with Candy Cain, how time stopped in the annex, and ended with inserting the watch key in the first portal.

I remove the remaining two timepieces from my pocket. "For whatever reason, I'm able to move these objects between worlds—the keys to closing down the last portals." I glance at the backwards running clock, and add, "We have twenty-five minutes left to deactivate them."

"You'll never do it by yourself," Slash touches my arm. "If I go, you'll be able to cut the time in half."

Jason taps out one thirty-minute immersion pill for Slash. I shake my head. "That isn't necessary. I can get us to the doorway of Time without it."

"How?" the director's brow furrows.

"I was told by the Traveler that all I need to do is visualize the doorway at the heart of time."

"I already know that." Jason cuts his eyes over to Slash. "What about him?"

I frown. "He doesn't have the latent ability to travel to the Hallway of Infinity like I do."

"So, what's your solution?"

"We'll form a psychic connection through our palm's minor chakra. When we hold them against each other's, Slash's mind will connect with mine. He will become a rider with me and project his astral body."

I pat the couch for Slash to sit down. "Jason, I suggest we quit talking and start doing."

I reach for Slash's hand and quickly form the mental connection. Before I close my eyes, I thank God that he is going with me.

Then, I fervently concentrate on our destination.

48

WHAT'S BEHIND DOOR
NUMBER TWO?

OUR PALM'S CHAKRA APPROACH TO THE Place Above
Time works. Both Slash and I now manifest in our astral
bodies in the Time Guardian's living room and wait as Mr.
Ed gets up from the couch. After a quick introduction to
Slash, the Time Guardian motions us toward the door leading to the Hallway of Infinity. We follow along, quietly,
with our own internal thoughts. Mine switch back and
forth. Would we save the alternate worlds and Earth? Or
would we fail? How had it come down to me, of all people
to do this?

I really question the gift I've been given.

Mr. Ed turns his head toward me as we hurry down the
corridor toward our destinations. I sniff the air to check for
more pot consumption and find none.

The Time Guardian stops in the hallway. "Archer, you've
closed the first opening Costas made in an alternate world,
the one that allowed him to loot its gold. Since the remaining two alternate worlds are still connected to your planet via
portals, the openings must be sealed in the next twenty-five
minutes, or both worlds and Earth will be destroyed."

I touch Slash's shoulder. "Do you want to shut down
the mental or spiritual breach?"

"Arch, I know you haven't been to church in over a decade. I'm afraid if you followed that destination, you'd erupt in spontaneous combustion. So, you take the mental domain."

I nod in agreement. "When you get inside the connected world, you'll find a circular portal linking them both. It's about seven feet tall, greenish colored, and pulses on and off. Because of your height, you won't have any problems inserting the key." I remove the two watches, match them up, and verify that they're the same. I hand one to Slash. "You want to insert the key in the hole at the top center of the portal." I emphasize the words, top center, and watch Mr. Ed cringe when he recognizes the wrong instructions, he gave me earlier.

The Time Guardian motions to the front of a nearby door. "This is the entrance to the mentally breached world." Mr. Ed glances at the pentagon-shaped timepiece. "You have twenty-one minutes to close the portal."

The Time Guardian grips the knob and opens it.

Slash crosses the threshold, winks at me, and starts to close the door behind him.

Mr. Ed moves around me, then sprints down the hall.

An eerie premonition raises the hair on my neck. The breath catches in my throat. I'm unable to move. I need one last glimpse of Slash to store up—just in case he doesn't make it back. I need one more kiss, and I need it now.

I blink hard to clear my vision. Why do I feel this is the last time I'll see him alive? Before I can warn him to be careful, the door closes behind him and the latch clicks in place. Slash vanishes into the dangerous world where everything is unsure, and death awaits.

49

THE BRAIN TRUST

MR. ED HOLDS THE DOOR FOR me. "After you."

I cautiously enter to close the second breach in the alternate world. Not knowing what to expect, I look to my left and see a small auditorium packed with folding chairs seating over one-hundred men and women. Each person has a metallic headband with suction cup sensors attached to the temple. A blue light, situated over the forehead, flashes on a few of the devices.

I feel the muted presence of the immobile bodies, and don't know what this is about, but I do know it's not good. Because no one moves. No one speaks. No one registers my presence. I am alive among the living dead.

A whisper of breath touches my arm and I look into the eyes of a middle-aged man beside me. There is a flicker of acknowledgement from him, and I intuitively reach for his headband. It comes off with a sucking sound as the temple contacts release. A thin line of blood oozes down his flesh and he sucks in air. Coughs violently.

"Are you all right?" I take his limp hand in mine. "I'm Archer. What's your name?"

"Tim. My name is Tim."

I wave my hand at the seated people. "What's going on?"

"He drained our minds." Tim's words are slow and painful. His face is a mask of horror now that he is aware.

I smell the acrid odor of nervous sweat and hear the raspy intake of air from the unconscious men and women. "What about the rest of them? What's wrong?"

"They're drained, too. All of them. Sucked dry."

There is a sea of people around us, a sea of hopeless faces, expressionless and slack.

Tim points to their headbands, "When the blue head-light is out, their consciousness is gone. In a few hours, they'll be dead."

"What does this do?" I hold the device up.

The corners of his eyes crinkle with pain when he touches his bloody temple. "Costas used our technology to drain every scientific advance our society has made. The cure for cancer, Aids, and Alzheimer's. Also, the secret to longevity and the source of unlimited renewable energy." He shakes his hand at his fellow scientists. "Then he left us to die."

From the corner of my eye, I think I see something skitter in the dark, at the back of the auditorium. But, after a second glance, there is nothing.

Tim points at the seven-foot portal connecting his alternate world with mine. "Damn him to hell. Costas captured all our learning and stored it in that device on the other side."

I glance through the portal and see the winking lights on a large super-computer. "Is the harvested information still in its hard drive?"

"No. Costas drained the last of the scientist's knowledge from its memory right before you came."

I pull out my pentagon shaped watch and check the time. Five minutes to go before imminent destruction. I quickly grab a nearby folding chair on my way to the portal.

So far, Costas has stolen billions of dollars of gold, as

well as priceless information in the form of specialized medical treatment and renewable energy technology. The third arena of exploitation is the spiritual realm. I know these three areas were not picked at random, but rather, as part of a larger plan. What that diabolical scheme is, only God and Costas know.

I place the folding chair next to the flashing portal and step onto the seat, watch key in my right hand. Just as I insert the time piece to close the portal, a dark mass streaks by, slams against my chair and disrupts my equilibrium. The shadow figure leaves the alternate world and jumps across the portal into mine.

"Oh my God!" I plunge to the floor and hit my forehead on the concrete.

Just as the portal closes, I have an intuitive flash—Slash is in imminent danger and something bad is about to happen. As blackness descends around me, I curse Costas for all the death and destruction he has wreaked upon me and pray it's not too late to help my lover.

50

IN GOD WE TRUST

AS SLASH CLOSED THE DOOR BEHIND him, he looked to his left and took a sharp breath. A majestic nebula shone in the infinite darkness of the breached alternate world. A swirl of celestial gas and dust glowed upon a background of magenta and royal blue, while a myriad of stars shone around the perimeter, adding to the spiritual presentation of God's creation.

Slash struggled against the vertigo that consumed him, feeling overwhelmed by the depth and breadth of Divine presence. He released his fear and a complete peace came upon him. One that spoke on a deeper level—Slash had reached the place his soul called home.

The nebula began to swirl faster until the field of gas, dust, and matter tightened to a brilliant dot of pure white energy. He stared in awe at the beauty around him, and the energy that illuminated the infinite space he stood in. Energy that presented a visual history of the alternate world's religions.

Slash absorbed the story of the origin, evolution, and attainment of this world's spiritual knowledge. Transfixed by the images, he watched the tales of untold numbers of men and women who were called by God to bring forth the message of love and peace. He observed the untold sacrifices made by those who answered the call and absorbed the untold stories of everyday people who believed in doing the right thing.

The celestial light dimmed, and Slash was aware of a dark energy coming from the other side of the portal. A cold, dismal light shone upon a lusterless throne, encroached by shadows. Coldness crept up his spine, and a voice Slash recognized, violated his bubble of spirituality.

Costas strode into sight. "Welcome to my greatest triumph, Slash. You're on hand to witness the birth of the next great religion. One where the masses will worship me as their Divine earthly ruler."

"You're nothing but a fat fucking freak with delusions of grandeur. What makes you think anyone would worship you?"

Costas crossed over the portal and put his hand in the air, displaying three fingers. "First, I have billions of dollars in gold. Second, I have the technology to change and extend lives. And third, thanks to the spiritual nebula you just experienced, I have the knowledge of how to manipulate the masses into believing I am God."

Slash shook his fist. "Your narcissism enhances your stupidity. Sane people already know that you can't buy or manipulate your way to being God. It's heinous!"

"History has shown that you can lead the masses down any path you can imagine. Look at Jonestown, Hitler's Third Reich, even the cult in Waco, Texas. I have the money, the technology, and the information to seduce people into accepting me as God. You of all people, are in no place to judge me."

Costas reached into his robe, withdrew his revolver. "I alone decide who lives and dies. I can give life and I can take it, Slash. You will be my first sacrificial lamb."

Slash dived for cover, but Costas anticipated the move when he fired. The bullet took Slash hard in the chest. He jerked from the impact, struggled to remain standing. He took a step and his legs gave way. Burning pain exploded across his chest. Hot blood gushed from his wound.

His breath came in ragged gasps and he prayed he would see Archer again. Just one more time to touch her face and tell her he loved her.

Costas now stood over him and removed the pentagon-shaped watch. "I'll close the last portal, Slash, and leave you in peace. Oh, and when you see Archer's parents in hell, give them my regards."

Slash held his hand against his bleeding wound and spit on Costas shoes. "If anyone will go to Hell, it's you." He gasped for air. "So, fuck off!"

Slash watched helplessly as Costas reached up, inserted the watch key in the top center of the portal and stepped back into his world. Before the door closed, he smirked. "If Archer finds you before you die, tell her she'll have to lick your spit off my shoes. Then, if she's any good in bed, I just might let her live."

51

THE WHITE LIGHT

SOMEONE SHAKES MY SHOULDER AND SHOUTS in my ear, "Are you all right?" I slowly come awake by degrees, remembering the dark mass that streaked past me and made me fall. After a glance at the auditorium and its muted occupants, I turn to Tim, who helps me up from the concrete.

It takes a few seconds to fully put it together. I touch a large knot on my forehead. "How long have I been out?"

"About two minutes, Archer."

I stand and sway slightly. Tim reaches out to steady me. I'm not ready to move. But move I will because my intuition hammers in my head that Slash is in danger. One shaky step follows another as I stumble toward the door.

I sadly look back at the auditorium of doomed scientists. I know they wait for no one, and no one but death waits for them. As I reach the door, I pray that Tim will survive. He gives me a feeble wave, as I step outside and into the Hallway of Infinity.

Mr. Ed is there for me, and I tell him what I need. He quickly leads me to Slash's door. I jerk it open to see my lover lying in a pool of blood next to the closed portal. I rush to his side and drop to my knees. Cradle his head in my arms, "Oh God. Please, don't let him die."

Slash's chest wound bubbles fresh blood with each exhalation, and his breathing is shallow. There is a sickening gurgle in his throat.

His eyes flutter open and my heart skips a beat. I tenderly brush back his hair. "I'm here Slash. Can you hear me?"

His upper lip pulls back, in Slash style, and my emotions take a dive. My prayer to God is simple. Let him live to be my future husband. Let him live to be the father of our children.

Dear God.

Please. Just let him live.

I bury my face against his neck and sob. I rock him back and forth while tears run down my cheeks. My life would be nothing without his grin, his wit, his arms around me, holding me, keeping me safe. If he dies, I won't have the strength to live. Slash is my rock, my North Star, my anchor. I whisper, "You can't die now. Slash, you've got to hang on."

Grief clutches my heart like an iron band, squeezes tighter with each breath Slash takes. As hope begins to fade, the broad, dark canopy of the universe above us, flickers, then brightens to a muted white. I look over my shoulder and feel its touch, like powdered sugar sprinkled upon my skin. Alive and aware, the light speaks in the language of spirituality. As it turns brilliant, pristine white, it speaks in the language of God.

Calming, lucent, and infinite, the living light forms into an ethereal ring that pulses with power. I look in Slash's eyes and see them begin to glaze over. I grip him fiercely. "You can't leave me Slash. Don't die on me!"

The circular band of light births a ghostly copy from its round mass, which rolls like a smoke ring, gently downward. Within its revolving borders, I sense the presence of the infinite as it lays its pearly essence over Slash.

He coughs. "Archer, do you remember that time… when you told me… your feet were cold?"

A piercing pain lodges in my heart, and I'm afraid to speak. Afraid I'll lose it completely. I nod my head, yes.

He coughs again. "That silly thing I did. You remember. I blew warm air on your feet, then said, 'there's nothing like warming your sole.'" Slash gasps for air. "Tell me what you said after that."

I look in his eyes. See his life ebbing away. My hands begin to tremble, and coldness surrounds me. "That's exactly what you do for me, you warm my soul."

I brush my lips against his, "Don't leave me. Don't go."

"Don't forget me Arch. I love you."

Slash takes a breath. Shudders. His life force, a fading hum. Then he is still. The Traveler's warning resonates in my mind, if the astral body dies, then the earth body does, too.

A white mist seeps from his torso. A living, moving, manifestation of his soul that slowly rises, then is absorbed into the white ring above us. I grip his hand. Press it to my lips. My lover, my soul mate is dead, and I will never be the same again. I straighten my shoulders and take a deep shuddering breath. I now face the bitter reality of a world without Slash.

Even in this moment of profound transition, anger over the pointless deaths of my parents and Slash, sends me into a fury. A keening sound escapes my lips and my anger escalates to rage.

I vow to pursue and exact revenge upon Costas and Le Cadavre. No matter where they run, no matter where they hide, they will pay for their crimes.

They will regret the day they ever met me.

52

I'M ELECTRIFIED

THE DAY AFTER SLASH'S MURDER, I'M in the Hallway of Infinity with Mr. Ed.

He opens his arms and gives me a hug. "I'm so sorry about Slash, Archer. But you have a duty to perform." He brushes his dark hair from his eyes. "Behind this door is Le Cadavre. I don't know what he is doing, other than it's early morning and he's in his apartment. When you go through the Hallway door, time will stop for everyone inside except yourself."

I put on a pair of latex gloves and slam a magazine in my Smith & Wesson 9mm semiautomatic. "It's time to clean house, Ed, and I'll start with the rats first."

The Time Guardian stands back as I open the door and enter Le Cadavre's apartment. The stench of rotting food hits my nostrils and I see molding pizza on the kitchen bar. A quick check confirms his absence in the living room, so I move to the bedroom. An unmade bed and a dirty pair of underwear confirm his presence. I open the adjacent bathroom door with the barrel of my gun.

There he is.

He has commandeered a doppelganger's body, but he's still the same son of a bitch who helped poison my parents.

He is sprawled out in a porcelain tub, taking a bath, with his head against the wall and his arms resting on the rim. I chamber a round and sight down the barrel. My finger tenses against the trigger. I empty my lungs, steady my hand.

Then, I remember the horrible deaths of my parents. Their escalating heart rates. The panic they felt. The explosion of pain before they died. My breath hitches in my throat when I recall pressing my lips against Slashes before he died.

No, Le Cadavre will not die easily. I lower my gun and go back in the bedroom, where I find a small radio alarm clock. I pick it up and reenter the bathroom, plug the cord in the wall socket and wedge the clock between his left shoulder and neck.

For my plan to work, he needs to jerk up and knock the clock off his shoulder, into the water. I dig a small Swiss Army pocketknife from my pants, open the three-inch blade, and ram it into his forearm.

I twist the knife from side to side, because when I leave here and time starts again, this will hurt like a bitch and he'll jerk in response.

When he does so, the alarm clock will fall in the tub.

Then, lights out, Le Cadavre.

I backtrack to the Hallway of Infinity and move into the corridor. I have decided to take retribution against him because he is beyond the law of earth while in an alternate world. My hand tightens on the doorknob, and I push it shut.

Inside his bathroom, time starts again, and an electrical explosion rattles the door, followed by a bloody scream.

In memory of my parents, and Slash, I take satisfaction in a job well done.

53

THE TASMANIAN DEVIL

I TURN TO MR. ED IN the Hallway of Infinity. "One piece of vermin down. One to go,"

He nods in affirmation. "Costas is present in his home, and when you enter, you can stop time."

I grind my teeth and say a prayer for my dead loved ones. Slash and my parents were killed, brutally and senselessly, and for that, Costas will pay the supreme price with his life.

This is something I must do because, legally, Costas is dead from committing suicide in Florida. And there is not a court in the world that would entertain the idea of prosecuting a free-floating consciousness that can travel between alternate worlds.

Costas has been a black eye for the psychic espionage program, and since he is officially dead, higher ups have discreetly given their approval for his removal.

The dirty work is getting ready to start as I open the door and step inside Costas' luxury home. I stand in a rich marble foyer and look over at an art deco wall clock—its hands frozen at 10 am. My gaze travels to the left, up the mahogany stairway, where I catch a glimpse of Costas, frozen at the top wearing a blue silk shirt and thin cotton shorts.

Like Le Cadavre, a bullet is too merciful for this scum.

I'm in no hurry to leave as I put on a pair of latex gloves. I wander into the kitchen, look around, and open the fridge. A typical man's assortment is inside—Chinese takeout and ten bottles of beer.

I don't know what I'm looking for, but my psychic antenna takes me through the kitchen, into a mudroom, and then through a door to the garage. Once there, I randomly open cabinets, just waiting for an intuitive flash. Nothing sparks my interest, so I walk over to a steel stand with gardening insecticide, rose fertilizer, and several lawn sprinkler heads.

Just as I'm about to leave, I recognize what led me here. When you have vermin to kill, you find the best way to do it. I grab a box of rat poison, a nearby hammer, and a gallon of antifreeze. I backtrack to the fridge where I get a plastic sack off the counter and put all the bottled beer inside.

A trip around the corner and I ascend the stairway. Then place the poison and beer four steps down from Costas. I mount the stairs until my face is level with his shoes. I lean over and tie his laces together. The memory of having done this before is now flavored with the seriousness of the occasion. I've come to kill him, not prank him.

Once the laces are tied, I step down and empty the beer bottles onto the foyer floor, then break them with the hammer. I'm careful to spread the broken glass evenly over the wooden stairs. It's my plan that when I leave, and time starts up again, Costas will fall from his tied shoes, and impact the five steps I've littered with broken glass.

But that's not all I have in store for the bastard. I open the box of rat poison and smile at the strychnine warning. I douse the crushed glass liberally with the powder and add a layer of antifreeze to round out the poisonous cocktail.

When Costas falls, two-thirds of his body will land

on the glass, puncturing and lacerating his flesh, only to introduce the rat poison and antifreeze into his bloodstream. His clothing will offer no protection from the broken bottles and will feed the toxic substances into his wounds as the material lies against his mutilated body.

With that thought in mind, I walk back to the doorway, look at Costas one final time and see a shadow move behind him. I jolt, and my heart skips a beat, until I look out the front window and see a tree swaying in the wind. The sun is behind it and casts a silhouette inside. So, I dismiss it as irrelevant and turn to leave.

When I close the door, time starts again. Inside, a body lands on hard wooden stairs. A horrible shriek lifts the hair on my neck. I take a deep breath.

All in all, it's been a good day's work.

ONE INSTANT, COSTAS WAS STARTING DOWN the stairs, and the next, he tripped and began to fall. In a flash, he saw the crushed glass on the steps below him. In his peripheral vision, he assessed a twenty-foot drop to the marble floor below. Costas' new, commandeered body weighed two-hundred pounds and even if he went over the rail, the fall would probably kill him.

Another microsecond and his thighs and calves were adrenalized—primed and ready to leap over the broken glass. He sprang into action, launched his body over the steps, felt the air upon his face, and started a trajectory above the deadly trap.

Costas looked down at the glistening, broken glass, smelled the antifreeze, and acknowledged a dark, grey powder upon the broken bottles.

A microsecond later, his right arm and torso hit the edge of the mahogany steps, barely missing the broken glass. The hard wood and friction took a layer of flesh from his arm and knocked the wind out of him. He curled in a ball and tumbled down the remaining steps, felt the pop of a broken rib, and screamed in rage as he hit the marble floor.

Costas slowly stood up and knew he was damned lucky. Lucky to be alive. The skin on his right forearm was bright pink and oozing blood, his broken rib hurt like hell. But the rest of him was miraculously intact.

He took a shuddering breath, removed his shoes, and looked back at the trap Archer had set for him. It had been close this time. Too close. It was way past time to take the bitch out. Archer wasn't the only one able to travel to alternate worlds. This time, Costas would bring a legion of mind-controlled killers with him and would obliterate Archer, leaving a bloody pulp in the wake.

The wind moved the trees outside, and Costas glanced up the stairway to see a black shadow moving slowly downward. The scratch and scuttle of animal claws on the stairs made his testicles retract in fear.

He rubbed his eyes.

Opened them.

The shadow now stood in front of him.

Primal fear punched a path through Costas' brain.

It was like nothing he'd ever seen. It was a man-sized blob of dark matter bristling with vicious looking quills. In place of its face was a large hole with glistening teeth, layered in rows that turned inward—allowing food in, but not out. The razor-sharp incisors moved and surged in anticipation. Saliva dripped on to the floor below, and the monster's feet clicked their razor-sharp claws against the marble.

Costas tried to move away from the creature but was pinned against the wall.

The thing didn't have lips or a tongue, however Costas heard it clearly, "Even though the multiverse is not in immediate peril. We find you guilty of past crimes—the loss of life and theft of resources, and commit your body to the ultimate punishment, death by ingestion."

Costas bolted for the front door. Fumbled with the doorknob, trying desperately to get it open.

The creature's quills bristled. Shot outward. Piercing Costas's back in a dozen places. He tried to run, but the barbed quills were still attached to the shadow monster. As it began dragging him back to its gaping mouth, a paralytic agent from the quill's tips froze Costas' muscles, and he dropped to the floor.

He tried to move his consciousness from this body but was blocked from doing so.

Costas was in mind-numbing agony and screamed as the dark creature dragged him to his death.

The retracting quills delivered his feet to the beast's waiting teeth. Teeth that moved upward and downward, drawing his body inside, breaking apart bone and muscle with a sickening crunch.

Another mighty scream erupted from Costas' throat. Horrific pain shot through his legs and thighs as the teeth shredded his bare flesh. The creature's mouth then expanded to accommodate the torso.

Before Costas' body disappeared, he pleaded for mercy. Pleaded for forgiveness.

And finally, he pleaded for death.

THE MOMENT HE DIED, THE POWERS that be acknowledged his execution and withdrew their enforcer from Costas' estate.

SCOTCH ANYONE?

THE COOL DIMNESS OF THE HALLWAY of Infinity hits me as I take a quiet walk with Mr. Ed to his apartment. My heart is heavy, my thoughts in a whirl. Where will I go now that I'm all alone? I can't face the emptiness of my life and a home I don't want to return to. No one waits for me there. No one cares or wonders about my absence. And no one can comfort me with a gentle touch.

Mr. Ed opens his apartment door and I notice we have a male guest. I wipe my tears away and straighten up. The visitor is short and round, has dark hair and wears a black pork-pie hat. There is a well-chewed cigar between his lips and a glass of scotch in his left hand.

He removes his hat. "I'm Johnny."

I nod and smile. "Archer."

Mr. Ed reaches down by the couch and picks up two duffel bags. "Well, it's been nice knowing you, Archer."

"Hey, what's going on here, Ed?"

The Time Guardian's face flushes and he turns his head down.

Our pudgy guest takes a sip of scotch. "Might as well tell her."

"Well, I made a couple of mistakes handling your use

of the facility. I almost sent you to Hell when I opened the wrong door in the Hallway of Infinity."

"And?" Johnny takes a sip of scotch.

"I didn't know where the watch key went in the portal."

Johnny smacks his lips, and chomps on his cigar. "We could'a had a real situation, Ed."

The Time Guardian's shoulders slump and sadness creases his face.

"I'm really sorry, Archer."

"You did the best you could. You got me where I needed to go."

"But things could'a gone wrong," Johnny adjusts his hat. "And that's why I'm terminating your employment here."

The Time Guardian glances around, avoiding eye contact, and I can tell this hurts him more than he wants us to know.

"Where are you sending me?" His voice catches.

"Someplace really cold."

Mr. Ed's hands begin to tremble. "Like in, as cold as hell?"

"I'm not sending you there, son, if that's what you mean."

Sweat pops out on Ed's brow and I reach over and pat his arm.

"Like I said," Johnny stabs his cigar to emphasize. "Someplace cold, but only in the winters."

The Time Guardian's face brightens up. "Then, where are you sending me?"

Johnny takes another sip of scotch. "How about your own marijuana dispensary in Denver, Colorado?"

A look of ultimate bliss fills the Time Guardian's face. Johnny shakes Ed's hand, and grins. "There's no drug testing, and I've already loaded $100K in your retirement plan."

Mr. Ed's mouth hangs open, and Johnny lights up his cigar, takes a few puffs and blows smoke into the Time Guardian's face.

I blink my eyes, and just like that, my friend is gone.

Johnny puts his hand on my shoulder, and I look into his dark eyes. "Just who are you?"

"With a little thought, you'll figure it out." Johnny takes a deep breath, and expands his barrel chest, then gently moves his hand to my arm. "You're in a transition phase, Archer. Your mother and father as well as Slash are gone. You're all alone. It'll take time to heal and this place will help you do so. Until you tell me differently, would you like to become my new Time Guardian?"

IN THE FIRST FOUR MONTHS SINCE I became Time Guardian, I kept too busy to do much thinking. My first change was to rip out the old shag carpet in the Apartment above Time. As well as repaint the walls and get all new furniture. A fresh set of room deodorizers has banished the cigarette and marijuana smoke, and the place now feels like home.

For months, I had ached with tremendous loss and experienced times when the loneliness washed over me in powerful, irresistable waves. My heart was battered, beyond repair. Even the distraction of my new job didn't fill the hole in my soul. The hole left by the deaths of my parents and Slash.

Then, I received a note from the Traveler, directing me to a door in the Hallway of Infinity. Over the last six weeks, I visited it many times. Today, I square off in front of the same door, take a deep breath, turn the knob, and think of Slash. He's the man I loved with all my heart and soul. He's the man I wanted a future with. He's the one who completed me. There is a stirring deep inside me as I enter a rather plain, middle-class living room. Six steps and I open the door to the patio outside.

Four people are on the deck, and they all acknowledge me with smiles and greetings. Dad, at the grill, asks, "One steak coming up, medium rare."

Mom hands me a glass of fresh-squeezed lemonade and kisses my cheek.

My gaze shifts to Slash and the big smile on his face. He opens his arms and I walk into his embrace, laying my head on his shoulder.

"I love you, baby." He kisses me on the lips, then steps back. He gets down on one knee and opens a small black velvet box. Inside is a sparkling, diamond ring. "Will you marry me, Archer Ann Wilson?"

I'm stunned. Can't form the word, so I just nod yes, like a fool.

He raises my right hand and kisses all five fingers. "I'm so glad your doppelganger agreed to let you meld with her."

I run my hand over his arm. "It's fortunate that I didn't need an immersion pill to allow my awareness to transfer. Since this Archer and I have the same measure of mental strength, there is no weaker consciousness to be absorbed by the stronger. But the real reason you're happy is because you're getting two wild women in bed."

Slash rolls his head back and laughs. "You're all I ever wanted Arch, so just call me grateful."

I place my hand on my stomach. "You have a lot more to be grateful for, Slash."

He grins back. "I know your secret."

"Get outta town. I just found out today."

Slash takes a sip of lemonade. "The sonogram showed a boy, didn't it?"

I brush my hand against his cheek. "Sometimes it sucks being engaged to a psychic."

"Well, if it makes any difference, our son will certainly have plenty of mentors," Slash motions toward my parents who have been engaged in a discussion.

Mom crosses her arms and leans toward Dad. "I told you last week that Archer was pregnant."

"Didn't I tell you the same thing, the week before that?"

Mom and Dad continue their mock argument and I'm totally happy. Mr. Ed told me months ago that if you can visualize something and think of your destination, you can go anywhere in the Hallway of Infinity. I'd forgotten that until my message from the Traveler.

So, I'd thought of a time before Costas' chaos and destruction and ended up in this alternate world. Here, I found my substitute parents, my alternative Slash, and an Alternate Archer who allows me to reside in her body.

I am blown away, my family and I have great emotional wealth, and my world is complete with those that I love.

It's forever. It's permanent. Aren't that what dreams are made of?

MICHAEL DAVID graduated from West Texas A&M in 1988 with honors, earning a BBA in Finance. For the next two years, he worked as an assistant examiner for the F.D.I.C. during the banking crisis of the late 80's. By that time, though, Michael had decided to heed the call of becoming a writer and quit his job in 1990. He found a job in Amarillo, Texas working with people with disabilities and began writing.

He is the author of five novels and two screenplays, and is currently under contract with publisher Oghma Creative Media.

Michael is now retired, and resides with his wife in Amarillo, Texas where he is an active member of the writing community.

MICHAELDAVIDAUTHOR.COM